Rope of Time

Rope
of
Time

a novel by
Larry Warwaruk

Cormorant Books

The publisher wishes to acknowledge the assistance of
The Canada Council, the Ontario Arts Council, the Saskatchewan
Arts Board, and the Multiculturalism Sector of the Department of
the Secretary of State.

The cover art is from an etching entitled *Jane* by William Laing,
courtesy of the artist and The Canada Council Art Bank.

The excerpts from *The Kalevala: Epic of the Finnish People* are
taken from Eino Friberg's translation, published by Otava Publish-
ing Company Limited in Helsinki, Finland, in cooperation with
The Finnish North American Literature Society, Inc. in Turku,
Finland.

The ballads in chapter four are taken from *The Oral Repertoire
and World View: An Anthropological Study of Marina Takalo's
Life History* by Juha Y. Pentikäinen, published by Suomalainen
Tiedeakatemia, Helsinki, Finland, in 1978.

Letter excerpts from the labour camp are courtesy of Jack Lahti of
Richmond, B.C.

Some of the labour camp images were derived from Alexander
Solzhenitsyn's *Gulag Archipelago*, Harper, 1974.

Printed and bound in Canada.

Published by Cormorant Books, RR 1, Dunvegan, Ontario, Canada
K0C 1J0

Canadian Cataloguing in Publication Data

Warwaruk, Larry, 1943-
    Rope of time

ISBN 0-920953-48-4

    I. Title.

PS8595.A786R66 1991   C813'.54   C91-090139-2
PR9199.3.W37R66 1991

To Mavis

Väinämöinen sailed, speaking,
And he said as he was leaving:
"Let the rope of time run out—
One day go, another come—
And again I will be needed.
They'll be waiting, yearning for me
To bring back another Sampo..."

Kalevala, Runo 50

Chapter One

Louhi, Pohjola's old mistress,
Uttered out the words which follow:
"I will only yield my daughter,
And my child I promise only
To the man who welds a Sampo
With its many-coloured cover."

Kalevala, Runo 7

Lempi enjoyed cleaning the room. Maybe because she did it so seldom. She cleaned the bedroom only when the young master was home from the University. How nice it would be to sleep in this bedroom.

The bed would be worth more than all her family's belongings in Kuusamo. Her father told her that working for a Swede would be a bed of down. She grinned. If her father could see this bed, she knew what he would say. He would say, "That's for Swedes." Her father would think it insulted the pride of a Finn to have something like this bed. "That's for Swedes to show off!" That is what her father would say.

"It's a monster!" Lempi laughed. "It wouldn't even fit in our hut at home."

Lempi bounced on the springs, then sprawled face-down, spread-eagled on the quilts and rubbed her cheek on the silk. She was only fourteen and she missed her family, but in these moments it was nice to be away from home. There was plenty to eat here.

Father said the bad times would come—that people shouldn't be fooled by the reign of the second Alexander. He said the czar would change his liberal tune. Lempi always enjoyed listening when her father talked in their house, smoking and drinking coffee with the men from the village. She remembered how her father had asked the men, why, when the frost shrivelled the rye kernels to nothing, the people should still be forced to pay money to the bishops. If it wasn't the Russian Orthodox bishop on a visit from St. Petersburg, it was the Lutheran landlord filling his pockets. For three years, what little rye there was, Mother had to mix with pine bark to make the famine bread. Lempi had helped her scrape the bark and she remembered the bitter taste of that bread.

The men from the village sought the help of her father. He was the spirit man, and could do many things. One day a boy came, his foot cut by an axe, and Father took him to the sauna. Lempi remembered filling the sauna barrel with water from the well, watching as her father mumbled, spitting on the boy's wound until its bleeding stopped.

One summer, a young couple, unable to bring a baby into the world, came to him. "Can you help us, Shaman?" they asked. He took them to the sauna, bathed them, and mumbled his words. Next spring the woman bore a child.

But Father could do nothing about the famine. At first he blamed the Swedes. He had heard twenty years ago about the Swedish Missionary, Laestadius, stirring up the Lapps in the northwest—the Great Awakenings at Kautokeino in 1860. And then these stirrings came to Kuusamo. Father resisted, but more and more the people were falling to these teachings and turning away from her father.

On the soft bed Lempi rolled onto her back and stared at the ceiling. The tax collector had told her father about the Nordholm's need for a domestic, and here she was. But she shouldn't loll about—there was work to do. She turned over on her stomach again, sinking into the quilt one last tiny moment, then twirled herself off the bed.

She polished the brass bed until the designs gleamed. Carefully worked trees, dogs, riders on horses jumping a stream, a darting fox with his head turned at the pursuers—all this raced in front of her as she polished the scene on the head of the bed.

"Do you like it?"

"Oh, you startled me. Yes, it is a nice picture."

"It is an English bed, and this is an English fox hunt." Olavi Nordholm looked up and down at Lempi. "Would you like to see where we Swedes go when we hunt?" he said.

Lempi hung her head. "I don't know," she whispered.

Olavi was on leave from his studies at the University at Helsinki, where for the first time, lectures were being given in Finn. He concentrated on Finnish language studies, and liked to practice on Lempi. She wondered why these Swedes tried to be Finns. He had even changed his name from Olaf to Olavi. He had told Lempi that for hundreds of years Finland was a part of Sweden, and only since 1809 had the Russians owned Finland. It was Olavi Nordholm's goal in life to make an independent Finland.

"Would you like to see our hunting lodge?"

"Oh." Lempi didn't know how to answer. The young man was far above her station. Why would he make this offer to a servant? But she was compelled by his ice-blue eyes, and it frightened her. Her hands shook as she straightened out the wrinkles her body had made in the quilts.

"Well?"

"If that is your wish," she said.

A sleigh waited outside. A boy, younger than Lempi, sat patiently, dwarfed in a heavy coat. Without letting go of the lines, he came down from the sleigh and stood at attention while Olavi seated Lempi.

Winding through the forest the sleigh rode cushioned on a new fall of snow. For a moment they stopped while the boy adjusted the horse's collar. Lempi looked at the trees. The birches glistened. Ice fragments tinkled, falling to the snow, as a sparrow, hopping to a branch, pecked at a brown leaf. On their way again, she heard the harness chains and the collar bells. *ching, ching, ching.*

They came to a clearing. The lodge, a big log building, stretched over the snow like a fortress. Two giant spruce trees stood at the front of the lodge, their branches weighted down with snow. When the sleigh stopped, Lempi stepped down and her feet sank deep.

"Come back for us tomorrow in the afternoon," Olavi Nordholm told the boy.

The sleigh pulled away. Olavi, standing between the two giant spruces, looked at the lodge. Lempi wondered what he was doing, and she tramped through the snow to get a look at his face. She couldn't know what he was thinking.

Feeling dizzy, her stomach queasy, she turned around and walked away from him. Around the corner of the lodge she took a deep breath, and the cold air inside her felt good. She could look after herself, couldn't she?

She heard him. "Let's go in and get a fire going," he said. "It will take a while to warm the place. No one is here—the caretaker has taken the hunting dogs to Oulu for breeding."

Lempi suddenly realized they were alone. What was it he expected? She stood at the side of the building. For a moment she studied the thick base of the chimney, half buried in snow, the hardened mortar squeezed between the stones.

She followed Olavi, watching his back, as they walked into the lodge. There was the fireplace—such a large room. Many could sit and be warmed by the fire. He took her to the other end of the building and showed her the kitchen and living quarters of the caretaker, then up some stairs on to a balcony where she could see down to the main room where the fireplace was. Along the balcony were many rooms, some for sleeping, Olavi told her, some for storage and things.

Olavi prepared the fire. The curls of oily bark ignited first, then the splints, and the flames climbed, the kindling snapping, fire wrapping the birch logs.

He had brought a lunch basket, even oranges—before she came to work at the Nordholms she had never seen an orange. She sliced the ham, and the white bread, slicing the loaf thin, for not often did Lempi get to eat anything baked with wheat flour. She drank some wine—she had never tasted wine in her life before, and she wasn't queasy anymore, wasn't nervous. Lempi nestled under a reindeer fur skin that was draped on the couch.

She rubbed the fur along her neck, and listened to the roar of the fire. Perspiration beaded on her forehead. She let the wrap slide to the floor, dropping it on Olavi where he lay on his back watching her. He sat up, reaching, touching her hair and her damp neck. He moved his hand along the length of her arm, pulled her, coaxing her body to him down on the reindeer fur. She thought his face looked oddly twisted. Lying beside him she looked over his shoulder to the log wall, saw the shadows of the fire bounce as he reached out and pulled hard at her waist.

The next day Lempi walked along the edge of the fir trees that rimmed the clearing at the back of the lodge. Her feet left jagged holes that gaped in an uneven line along the trees. She pushed through the snow, wishing she could somehow push everything away, back to where she had been the day before, making beds. She grabbed a branch and snow shook down on her, melting on her face. With her strong hands she tugged at the bough until it ripped, and then she thrashed it back and forth, faster and faster in the snow. Then she dropped the branch and stood motionless, for a long time.

Olavi Nordholm watched from a window in an upstairs room.

It was an early summer afternoon when Olavi approached her in the Nordholm library. She was alone, dusting the books, and the brass ornaments on the fireplace mantle.

"The cook told me you are going to have a baby." He spit the words at her. "What is this all about?"

"I—I don't know."

"You have been messing with the stable boy. I saw that day how he looked at you on the sleigh."

"That night at the lodge...." Lempi whispered, and looked at the floor. Surely he knows, Lempi thought.

"That night at the lodge? You want me to swallow such a coincidence?"

He turned his back to her.

She felt hot. She squeezed the dust rag in her shaking hand. For weeks her guilt had pressed on her. At sudden moments, like hot flashes, the sweat would pour from her skin. She had no feeling for him other than a fear that somehow she had taken something from him, had something he owned, and he would want her or the baby.

"Yes, maybe I am, maybe I am with child," Lempi said, and she lifted her head to look him in the eye, but he had turned away.

"I have talked to my father," Olavi said. "We are sending you home, Lempi. The boy can take you to Oulu. We can't have these things going on with the servants. I will send a letter with the boy to arrange a boat for you from Oulu. At the warehouses there will be empty boats going back up river to Kuusamo." He placed a ten Krona gold-piece on the mantle-piece and left the room.

Lempi was the only female passenger on the boat. She wanted to lose herself in the water journey and make it last forever, but the slower she wished the shore to pass, the faster it went. She sat low in the boat facing three boys a year or two older than herself. Embarrassed, she pulled her birch bark pack to her lap. Then she set it down on the bench beside her, pulling her smock away from her belly.

Surely these boys knew just by looking at her, but they said nothing. All three smelled of turpentine—they had streaks of tar in their fair hair, and their shirts and pants were gobbed with tar. They were going for Mid-summer, to be home in time for solstice. They said that after a few weeks, maybe five or six, or whenever they felt like earning a penni, maybe they could river-log back to Oulu. One boy said he was going to help his father do the burning at his tar pits in the forest. All three would spend the winter at the tar works in Oulu again.

Three times the boat stopped at a mooring. Each time one boy got off and disappeared on a forest path. On the third morning, Lempi climbed from the boat. From the shore she watched as a dark-skinned Lapp loaded reindeer hides onto the boat, and then she walked into the forest. She followed a wet footpath to where it crossed a swamp. Logs were laid side by side, and as she walked on this bumpy path it moved under her. On each side stunted pine trees swayed back and forth in a low-lying fog, a gray-blue haze covering the floor of the swamp. With every step she took, the bog moved. She felt herself reeling like the pines. What if she stepped off the logs into this green sponge? She would sink into it and be gone. She would not have to face her father. What would her father say? I'll have to tell him, won't I? Won't he wonder why I'm home? Lempi broke into that same cold sweat. No, she could do it—she could face her father. She looked straight ahead at the log footpath, keeping her eyes off the bog. And hurried.

She came to the hay meadow, sensing for the first time that this was it. She was close to home now. Instead of climbing over the fence, she crawled between two rails, and with her belly in the way, strained to get through. Below her on the wet moss of the bottom log, a black slug inched slowly along.

The fence wound along the perimeter of the meadow, surrounded by a mixed forest of alder, aspen, birch, and spruce. The early summer leaves rippled, changing colour from silver to green, again and again. Further in the distance, lighting on the top branches, swaying, then hopping from branch to branch, seven ravens squawked loudly. Then she noticed the huts. There were too many of them to be shelters for the hay-cutting. She heard the ravens again. As she drew closer she noticed that beyond this grass hut village, in a smaller clearing behind a grove of spruce trees, hundreds of people had congregated.

"Lempi! Lempi!" Her brother, Tenho, raced towards her, shouting, "Lempi, you are here! The grace of God is upon us! The grace of God is upon us!" He grabbed her shoulders, tried to look into her eyes, but she lowered her head.

"What are you shouting?" Lempi said, forcing her head back up. She could see that he was not himself, that he was overcome with joy. His eyes gleamed.

"We are bathing in the blood of the lamb," Tenho said. "Everyone awakens to the Living God. Father has repented, and the grace of God is present. Come, Lempi, Father is speaking!"

Tenho pulled his sister into the crowd, her people, sturdy men in washed home-spun, flaxen-haired young women in sun-bleached smocks, fat women in dark dresses, scores of children. Beneath a canopy of neatly-fashioned spruce boughs, her father stood on a platform set against the forest wall of evergreens. He waved his fingers up and down, held the crowd with his eyes.

"It is as Laestadius said, as Luther did before him—to receive grace, one must first weep and lament as did the disciples when the Saviour died."

Lempi listened. She knew little from the Bible, though the Nordholms had required that she join with the other servants for Bible study on Sunday afternoons. Father's words covered her, smothered her like a blanket, as if these words of sorrow and forgiveness were for her only. Surely he couldn't have seen her in the crowd.

"The disciples had at first to sink into unbelief and hopelessness," he said, thundering the message.

Beside Lempi, two weeping men embraced. All over the place hands rose in the air. "Praise the Lord! Praise the Lord!" people shouted.

"At that moment when the sinner is deepest in despair—if he can then believe that all sins are forgiven through Christ, then, like a great dam bursting, the sins will wash away and you will have overwhelming joy that only true believers experience in the presence of the Lord!"

He paused, and slowly, from a single voice somewhere in the crowd, a hymn began, joined by other voices until the meadow rang with the music—*A Mighty Fortress Is Our God.* Lempi felt the weight of her sin, heavier and heavier. She hated herself, feared her father's retribution. Tenho placed his arm over her shoulder. "What is the matter, Lempi?"

She burst into tears. "Can't you see?" she sobbed, and clutched at him. "I'm to have a baby." Tenho's eyes filled with tears—his face reddened, and he squeezed her arms.

"Believe your sins forgiven, Sister. Believe! Believe!" She wailed. Out of control, her arms waving wildly, she ran through the crowd to her father. "Forgive me, Father," she yelled. He saw her. Her father came down from the platform. "I have sinned!" she sobbed. Her father held her in his arms.

"So you have come home," Lempi's father said later that evening in the quiet of his log dwelling. "Maybe that is good. Ever since your mother died, the fish soup has suffered. It needs a better cook." His deep-set eyes flashed, and he winked. "I will like to have you at home," he said, "and also the baby."

With peace in her heart she was happy to be back with her father. He did need a housekeeper—someone to scrub the floor, wash his clothes. What do men know? Besides, Tenho was always off somewhere. Lempi's father said that Tenho was starting a farm somewhere beyond the hay meadow.

Lempi spent the final weeks of her confinement alternating between housework and learning to read from her father's bible. When her time came, a mid-wife took her, and she was gone for three days. When she returned, it was with a baby boy.

She stood in the doorway and waited for her father to notice. For a long while he did not look up from his table; he read in halting words from his bible, and only when he completed the passage, and satisfied himself that he had made progress in his efforts at learning to read, did he put the bible down and glance towards her.

"Will you name him for me, Father?" Lempi stepped, hesitatingly, part of the way to him. He met her, took the bundle, unwrapped it and examined the child, hands and feet.

"Ya, a strong boy. He will have to be strong, born in this time of soul struggles. Let us name him for these battles. Let us name him, 'Taisto'...'Struggle.' That is what we will name him.

He gave the baby to Lempi and sat down, looking closely at his daughter. "Ya, Lempi," he said. "There is something I wish to ask."

"What is it?" With the baby on her arm, and the coffee pot in the other hand, she filled her father's cup, then sat at the table across from him, putting the child to her breast.

"We are followers of Christ now," he said, "grace beggars. What gifts we have, we have from Him."

"Yes," Lempi said.

"When I was Shaman I had powers, Lempi."

"Yes."

"Can it be that God had given these powers to me?"

"All comes from God," Lempi said.

"Then He will pass the powers through me to you, Lempi. I know of healing plants, medicines from the forest, mushrooms, herbs. I know how to heal the body in the sauna—massage, and the blood-letting—*kuppaus*.

Secrets of the Shaman my father passed to me, I will pass to you, and we will sing together from *Kalevala*. Tenho is too impatient—he would not take the time. You stay with me, Lempi."

The father did not look at his daughter. His arms over the table, he leaned forward, and with his knife he cut thin shreds from a loaf-like slab of tobacco leaves. Seemingly concentrating on this sole task, he cut, then held the knife still, its edge poised on the wood. "You stay, Lempi, here, with the little baby. In time, this Taisto will grow to be a man. It will take time to show you these things, but you will learn. You are like me, Lempi."

They looked at one another, each with deep-set brooding eyes.

Yes, Father," Lempi said. " I am like you. I will be a healer."

Chapter Two

"Bridegroom, my most precious brother!
You have waited long, wait longer!
Your desired one is not ready,
Lifelong partner not prepared:
Only half her hair is braided
And the other half is braidless.

Bridegroom, my most precious brother!
Long you've waited without tiring;
Your desired one now is ready,
And your duckling quite prepared:
Go along now, dowered maiden,
Chick whose bride-price has been settled,
Now your union is at hand
And your time of parting near,
With your bridegroom by your side,
With your taker at the door,
Stallion champing at the bit
While the sleigh is waiting for you."

Kalevala, Runo 22

Lempi was young, but not young. She lived at home on her
father's acres, but not in the way of the maiden daughters she
loved to sing about in the *Kalevala*. She was not a maiden, not
a *"flower in the laneway"*, no longer was she *"like a strawberry
in a clearing"*, no longer *"a leaf that fluttered"*, *"meandered
like a butterfly"*, *"as a raspberry in a meadow"*, *"berry in her
mother's garden"*.

　　After Lempi's brother Tenho migrated to America,
and after her father died, Lempi and her son moved beyond the

meadows to her brother's vacated farm. Tenho had sold the land but kept the cottage and yard for Lempi. When the boy Taisto came of age he worked on the Lutheran Bishop's farm near Kuusamo.

It was the Christmas season, and Taisto with his new friend, Matt Inhonen, caught a ride on a fish pedlar's sledge all the way to Kuusamo. From the village Taisto and Matt walked through the trees and frozen meadows on the way to Lempi's cottage.

Taisto was lean, and he had a stiff, but determined gait. The nose on his sour face jutted like a hawk's beak aimed at his feet, raising upward now and then as if to peck at the snowy mists that clouded the division between the sky and the tree-line at the far end of the meadow.

"Ya," he said, more to himself than to Matt, "This country—only good for the owls. It is mid-day and still like night." He ground his teeth, clenched his jaw and thrust out his chin. "No wonder the bear sleeps all winter." He took off his leather mitt, held a finger to the side of his nose, and blew. He wiped his woolly coat-sleeve across his face. "Bah! I stink like a fish," he said in a low, grunting voice.

"Ya," Matt said, laughing quietly at Taisto's pessimism, "What is better, the fish, or trying to walk in this snow up to our knees? Ya, it would be good to have skis."

"I thought somebody might be hauling hay from the meadow, but no such luck." Taisto cursed quietly under his breath. "What good is this country? To get anywhere, a man needs a sleigh in the winter, and a boat in the summer."

They got to the other side of the hay meadows, crossed through the pine forest where the walking was better, and came to the lake. Through the snow mist, Taisto saw Lempi on her knees chopping with an axe, her water buckets and wooden yoke beside her on the ice. She didn't notice the men approach behind her.

"Hello, Mother," Taisto said. Lempi turned with the axe raised and Taisto took it from her. She held her hands to her cheeks.

"*Voi! Voi!* Taisto!" she said, rising, brushing snow from her skirts. "Why do you scare your mother?" Taisto laughed and chipped around the hole in the ice, dipped the pails, and slung them on the yoke over his shoulders. "Bring the axe, Matti," he said.

Lempi glanced only for a second at Taisto's companion, and then she and her son walked the fifty yards up hill to her cottage. Matt shrugged and followed them, carrying the axe. Lempi took the axe from him and hung it on the smoke-blackened wall by the door, beside a copper pot. She unbuttoned her home-spun woollen waist jacket and hung it on a peg, then filled the pot to boil coffee, put butter and flat-bread on the table.

"Mother, this is Matt Inhonen," Taisto said, breaking off a piece of the bread, and spreading the butter with his knife. "He worked with me in Helsinki."

Lempi nodded, gestured for this muscular young man to sit, and then she withdrew to the hearth to build up the fire. This Matti is a handsome man, she thought, glancing over. He has the blue fire in his eyes like my father had. She smiled to herself and shook her head—ya, he must be ten years younger then she was, and an unbeliever. How foolish of her to think him handsome. Ya, the flesh is weak, sometimes so eager. When she was younger, some men were interested in her, even with the baby, but she was not interested in those men. She would have preferred someone strong like her father, but such men were few, and maybe they didn't want her with the baby. She watched Matt, a strange man, eyeing her wood-carvings— the weasel and the cuckoo bird, on the beam above the door. Lempi stared at Taisto. "What about you?" she said. "What have you learned all that time in Helsinki?"

"So much is happening now in the 20th Century, Mother. Matti is *Social Democrat,* and he plans to go to America, maybe this spring, maybe next."

"America?" Lempi said, "that is a bad place—worse than Helsinki."

Matt blinked—a nervous blink. "But first we have to

get you married off, ya Taisto?"

Taisto blushed.

"What is this?" Lempi said.

"Didn't I tell you, Mother? When I cut hay for the bishop there was this girl from Oulanka, this Senja. We have written letters. Matti has come to speak for me. Maybe you will come with us to Oulanka—you know the old ways. But let's not worry about this now. The wedding won't be till March."

Lempi didn't know what to think, one surprise after another. Of course she would go with them, and she wouldn't worry about this now, she wouldn't worry at Christmas about her son marrying in March. It is good to take one thing at a time. She can have the winter with her son at home.

And for Taisto, what could be better for him than to spend the winter in his mother's warm cottage? He could sleep like a bear, eat the good fish soup from the iron kettle, pike heads and all. Why should he spend another winter freezing in the shipyards?

But she knew that with three people cooped up all winter, the nights would be long. Maybe she could tell her stories. This Matt might like to hear some of that *Kalevala,* even if he is a *Social Democrat.*

One afternoon, when it was already dark outside, Lempi was churning butter. The room was lighted by two pitch-covered splinters stuck in the wall above her head. She stood at the churn, her big hands on the handle of the plunger. Up and down it went, *splish, splish, splish.* Over and over, *splish, splish, splish,* and all the while, Lempi hummed softly.

Taisto sat on a bench, whittling a stick, and smoking an old pipe Lempi had given him that had belonged to her father. Matt stared trance-like at the fire.

"Ya, Mother, sing to us from *Kalevala,*" Taisto said. "I remember, when Grandfather was alive, you sang together all the time."

"Tonight, after I finish this butter." Lempi said.

Throughout the night Lempi sang. She chanted without stopping, as if her soul had left her body and hovered about the room. "*Väinämöinen*...." She droned in rhythms, on and on, about the birth of the world and *Väinämöinen*. The long, warm vowels stretched even longer, her utterances deep and low, haunting, verse after verse. "He was the father of all Finland, son of the virgin of the air, and fathered by the ocean." Lempi rocked back and forth on her bench. She told how *Ukko*, ruler of the heavens, sent a bird, a humble teal, not the greatest, not the smallest. The teal rested on the thigh of the virgin of the air as she floated on her back in the ocean. The two young men stared at Lempi's face.

Water-mother, maid aerial,
Felt it hot, and felt it hotter,
Then she jerked her knee with quickness,
And her limbs convulsive shaking,
Rolled the eggs into the water
And to fragments they were shattered.
From the cracked egg's lower fragment
Now the solid earth was fashioned."

They learned that from the egg fragments came the sky, and the clouds. The sun came from the yolk, and the moon from the white of the egg. They listened to Lempi's story of the birth of *Väinämöinen*, all through the creation, in the womb of the water-mother:

"Väinämöinen, old and steadfast
Rested in his mother's body
For the space of thirty summers,
And the sum of thirty winters,
Thereupon he moved the portal,
With his finger fourth in number,
Opened wide the bony gateway,
Headlong in the water falling."

Taisto felt the power of his mother's trance. He shook his head. He had this picture of *Väinämöinen*, an image of a mariner, a sword in one hand, and in the other a rudder pole braced over his knee. The sailor's white hair and waist-length beard streamed in the wind. *Väinämöinen's* girded rawhide smock was damp with ocean spray. Beneath his arched and bushy eyebrows, *Väinämöinen's* hard eyes glared at the sky. Much of the time Matt gazed into the fire, but Taisto fixed his eyes on his mother. She sang how *Väinämöinen's* marriage proposal was rejected by *Aino*, Virgin of Finland:

"Then her shift she cast on willows,
And her dress upon the aspens,
Stockings on the marshy ground,
Shoes upon a launder-stone,
With a rock the maiden Aino
Sank beneath the water's surface.
There the dove forever vanished,
Like a bird by death o'ertaken."

Taisto turned his head, back and forth, working his fingers into the muscles of his neck. He stood up. From a box beside the fireplace he took new splinters, lit them on a nearly extinguished stub, and stuck the lighted splinters high on the wall. He sat down again, facing Lempi who rocked on her bench. The shadows from the lighted pitch flickered on her face and on the wall behind her. She sang of *Joukahainen,* young god of the Lapps who came on his sledge to battle *Väinämöinen*. On the packed and narrow path their sledges met. Which would move aside for the other? Surely age must be respected, but *Joukahainen* would not budge. Who was the wiser? Who could out-sing the other? For days, each sang of his exploits. Finally, *Joukahainen* knew he was beaten.

Story after story she sang from the *Kalevala*. It was good, she thought, for the men to learn what it is to be a Finn. At times during the long winter, Taisto's mind wandered, thinking about starting a farm with the young Senja, or perhaps going with Matti to the golden streets of America. But some things from Lempi's singing slowly etched in his mind— images of the ancient Finnish gods, repeated many times in the *Kalevala* story. Of course there was *Väinämöinen,* father of these heroes. Then *Kullervo,* the warrior. Lempi wasn't sure that she liked *Kullervo,* but he was part of what it was to be a Finn. Kullervo left his parents' home and went to slaughter the people in *Louki's* kingdom. A messenger came to tell him that his father had died. There is a horse at home, *Kullervo* said. Let the horse drag the corpse to the grave. A Finn must do what he must do. When *Kullervo's* bloody deeds were done, he returned home. The ashes in his mother's hearth were cold, and all the family dead. On his sword, *Kullervo* killed himself.

But most important for Lempi was *Illmarinen,* father of blacksmiths. *Illmarinen* forged the *Sampo,* the magic mill built for *Louhi,* goddess of the Northland. When Lempi chanted about the blacksmith it was as if she lamented for the fate of the world. She sang of how *Illmarinen* looked into his forge to see his creation:

> *A crossbow thrust up from the fire,*
> *Bow of gold with silver tips,*
> *Shaft embossed with copper figures.*
> *Every day it claims a head,*
> *On its best day even two.*
> *So he broke the bow in pieces,*
> *Shoved the remnants in the fire.*

From the forge fires *llmarinen* rejected not only the crossbow, but also a boat, a red boat, whose purpose was war. No, he thought, the *Sampo* must not be for war. What would the *Sampo* be? Finally it rose from out of the fire and *Illmarinen* set to work with his hammer and tongs. A mill he forged, with a cover of gold, etched with doves and stars and coiling snakes around the rim, its ciphered cover spinning, grinding binfuls every morning, things to eat, things to sell, things for home. He took it to *Louhi.*

Mistress Louhi, overjoyed,
Had the magic mill carried
To the Northland's great Rock Mountain;
Hid it in a cliff of copper
And behind nine locks secured it,
Where it struck its roots down deeply
To the depths of fathoms nine

Ya, Lempi thought, and always it will be that men will chase across the world for this *Sampo.*

One morning Matt Inhonen walked to Kuusamo to get some newspapers, or, if for nothing else, to get out of the house for a day or two. Also the time was nearing for the wedding. He would see about borrowing a sleigh from the fish pedlar. Taisto and his mother went walking by the lake—a time of change was approaching for them both.

"You see these tree stumps?" Lempi said. "You wouldn't remember much of Uncle Tenho. The logs of my house were the trees he cut here. I never told you—it is by this place that Tenho's wife and the little boy drowned."

Taisto brushed snow off a stump and bade his mother sit. "Tell me what happened," he said.

Lempi sighed, opened her cloth bundle and laid out bits of hard bread and several dried smelts. "A terrible accident. Tenho had been cutting hay in the meadow. His little Ruth came running to him, crying, screaming about falling in water. She led him back here, showed him the bodies, here in the lake. Maybe the boy fell in—it's deep water close to shore. Who knows what could have happened."

"Did he go to America then?" Taisto chewed at the leathery fish, then took a bit of bread.

Lempi watched him eat. "No, Tenho knew nothing about America. It was in Norway he learned about America. The winter following the drownings, leaving Ruth with us, he skied north around the Gulf of Bothnia, through Kautokieno where Laestadius was. He tried to farm off the Bothnian shore, but the land was either swamp, or gravel piles.

"Some Finns had been there for centuries. He dug pits to collect the water, carried fish guts and seaweed to mix in the gravel to make soil. The Norwegians must have thought the Finns were crazy."

"How did he get to America?"

"Copper mines—there were copper mines in Norway, and, I guess, copper mines in America. Some Finns from the Norway mines were already going to America. Tenho heard from them."

"And then Ruth joined him in America?"

"Ya, when Tenho had enough money to send for her and she was old enough to travel by herself."

Taisto finished eating, and Lempi picked at the remains, then tossed crumbs to the sparrows hopping on the snow. "You know, Taisto, in America, Tenho is a speaker brother in the church. Something tells me you will go to America."

"Ya?"

"Maybe you will see him. Wouldn't that be something."

"No. I will farm here," Taisto said.

The following evening, Matt returned. "I talked to the fish pedlar," he said, and then paused, sitting at the fire chewing on a stick. Taisto paced back and forth in front of the hearth.

"Well? Well?" he said.

"Ya, we can borrow the sleigh, and no, not the fish sledge. You don't have to worry. It's a proper sleigh with leather seats. He has some land for sale too, not far from here. I told him you were interested. He says to talk to him when we come for the sleigh."

Lempi carefully attached three bells to the horse's collar. As they sped across the lake, the bells tinkled light and clean. Lempi said that was a good omen. If the sound had been muffled, for sure Taisto wouldn't get a bride.

It seemed to Lempi that her son was old for nineteen.

She watched as he leaned forward on the padded leather seat, how he peered to the side, staring across the crusted surface of the lake. She wondered what he was thinking. He never changed his expression—always the jaw was clenched, as if ready to spring, and every once in a while it did. His chin shot forward, then clicked back into place, as if he had decided something.

So he wants to be a farmer. He must have hoarded every meagre Nicholas *penni* from his wages to make the down-payment. Why did he pay it? What has he bought? Rocks, sand, trees, and swamp water. He wasn't the first to buy that piece of land. Three times the fish pedlar has sold it, and always he has it back to sell again. Taisto knows that. Why does he think he can do what three others before him couldn't? I should have said something. But no, it's not my business to pry.

"When we get to the village we must first find lodging," Lempi said. "Then ask where to find this Senja. Remember, it is Matt who must ask. The groom says nothing."

"Ya," Taisto said. "But look, look, there is Oulanka."

The village stretched along the shore—open country and low hills beyond the houses. Each unpainted dwelling, with cattle shed attached, stood apart from the others. The air smelled of woodsmoke. A white Orthodox Church, with blue trim and a golden dome with a separate bell-tower, sat on a hill up from the shore. Youngsters stood by a well.

"We have come from Kuusamo," Matt shouted. "Can anyone show us the dwelling place of Senja, daughter of Vilho Jukola?"

The girls giggled and hid behind the well. Two little boys ran up to the sleigh and stood gaping at the visitors. A tall boy stepped forward and pointed to a dwelling sunk back into a cover of scrub pines.

"And where can we get lodging, and something to eat?" Matt asked. The gaping boys pointed to the inn, and the tall boy grinned and nodded his head.

Two hours later, Matt knocked on the plank door of the Jukola dwelling. It was Senja who opened the door. She held a skein of hemp straw in her hand, and quickly set it aside along with a carding brush. A black skirt with a white linen apron hung down to her boots. A grey long-sleeved blouse gathered at her neck. Her cheekbones glowed. Her eyes glistened. Her hands played with a golden braid peeking through from her headscarf.

"We have walked far," Matt said. "Can you give us a drink of water?" He followed the unwritten script of the ritual to the word.

She led them into the dim smoky room. Two logs, a foot apart, ran side by side from the door to the far end of the dwelling. Fire burned along the inside of the logs near the middle of the room. Smoke rose to a hole high on the back wall. The men sat on one side of the logs, the women and children on the other. The smoky light flickered from a burning cedar splinter stuck in the wall above three men seated at a plank table. They appeared to concentrate on their tin coffee cups.

Senja offered Taisto a dipper. He drank. One of the men took a lump of sugar and placed it in his mouth. The man had a raised scar on his left hand. He sipped coffee through the sugar. The others did the same. Taisto handed the dipper to Senja and nodded. She blushed.

"I'll throw my mittens on the end of the beam," Matt said. He didn't do anything with his mitts—just said the words as Lempi had told him. The family would know Taisto was returning. The family needed time to consider.

The next day, just as Matt approached the three men, a burning piece of ash fell from a splint onto the table. The man with the raised scar brushed it to the floor. Matt spoke to this man.

"We are men from beyond the sea, involved in the matter. May we speak?"

"Strangers have spoken here before," the man said.

"To us has been born, Taisto Maki, son of Lempi. To you has been born a girl, Senja, daughter of Vilho Jukola. Shall we not become kin? Bring our two young people together?"

The man didn't speak, didn't move. His eyes were fixed on his tin cup.

"We ought to know what you think." Matt turned to Senja.

Senja eyed Taisto, then knelt at her father's knee. "Father, you have fed me and given me drink. Tell me what you think."

"If my advice is asked," the father said, without moving his eyes, "then I say we have enough food and drink at home. You need not go."

Senja rose, and sat in a dark corner beside a toothless old woman. Matt spoke again, the words strained and halting. "Should not these two be brought together?" The father would not budge.

"Give me your gracious permission," Senja said, again at her father's knee. "I shall go!"

Still the father did not move.

Matt and Taisto left the house.

They returned a third time the next evening and repeated the ritual. Finally, the father turned to his daughter and said: "May God have mercy. May God help you over lands and waters as you go. May God help you."

The father rose. His two table companions stood behind him, and his wife, and the others in the room—even the toothless old woman. Soot fell from above, as a boy crawled on the centre beam, coughing from the smoke and looking down. Matt and Taisto faced the group. Taisto reached for the hem of his woollen coat and held it in his right hand. The father did the same. They shook hands—but flesh did not touch flesh.

"We seal the transaction," Matt said. He pointed at Senja, then Taisto. "These will become one. Is there a listener?"

"I hear," the boy said from the roof, and he rapped a stick on the beam.

"The contract is complete then," Matt said. He tossed a coin up to the boy who reached out and caught it.

The inn was made ready for the wedding. Village women scrubbed the floor-planks, washed the tables, swabbed the benches with water. Lempi helped the older women prepare the salted salmon, roasts of pork, and creamcakes. One of Senja's uncles bought a barrel of ale from the Innkeeper.

Senja was at home. She sat on the pinewood chest her father had made, a chest such as he made for all his daughters. Senja's sisters, aged sixteen, fifteen, and seven, fussed around her. The youngest stood with her hand reaching out to touch Senja's dress. The older girls laughed. They combed and plaited Senja's hair. Today her mother did not burn splints. She lit her finest white candles, and the toothless old aunt cackled from her bench in the dark corner. Her face, leathery and withered like a slice of dried apple, was hidden by her shawl. She began her lament:

> *"Hast thou never, youthful maiden,*
> *Looked beyond the present moment,*
> *When the bargain was concluded?*
> *All thy life thou must be weeping,*
> *And for many years lamenting.*
> *Thou wast fond of bridegroom's money,*
> *Glad to have the chain he offered,*
> *But your home you now are leaving,*
> *To the household of a stranger.*
> *Not for one night you are going,*
> *You for months and days will vanish,*
> *Lifelong from your father's dwelling."*

Senja's father entered the room, and the old woman stopped her singing. The sisters stepped back from Senja, and her father took her by the hand. Slowly, father and daughter walked around the pinewood chest, and the old aunt resumed her lament:

> *"Long-tailed duckling, you should rather*
> *Walk with bare feet in the sea,*

Than to circle with your father round
The wondrous chest he gives you."

As he pulled her by the hand Senja could see her father's raised scar throbbing. They walked around the chest and then her father stopped, and he kicked at the corner of the chest. Again they circled and again he kicked.

On the third kick, he dropped Senja's hand, and sat at the table, lit on this day with candles. Senja knelt at his knee. Her two sisters placed a woollen three-cornered cap on her head, and let the veil fall over her face.

Senja's tears came when she felt the grip of her father's hand as they circled the chest, when he stopped the first time and pondered before kicking the chest. Maybe it was then she felt her father's anguish. She could feel his wish to give something of himself, give the pinewood chest, that he might be remembered.

She hadn't meant to cry. To this point the wedding was exciting to her. She didn't know why, all of the sudden, she was overcome. Maybe it was the laments of her auntie. Maybe she cried because she was happy and her sisters were happy—how excited they were for her.

Senja thought the saying of her words would be a mere recitation, but when she said them, at her father's knee, she felt each word, and the phrases came only in halting gulps.

"Can you , my precious good one,
Give table-clothes to your duckling
Who is going to outside strangers,
And can you, my precious good one,
Give towels whitened on hay poles
To your radiant duckling,
As I go to outside strangers.
And listen yet, my good one,
Can you give blankets to your duckling
As I go to outside strangers?
In Anger they might drive me

Out into a storm—then I will
Wrap myself in my parents' blankets."

The horse's bells could be heard from outside—the groom had arrived. Senja's father rose, and led her to the door. Matt and Taisto waited in the sleigh to take the bride to the golden-domed church for the wedding ceremony required by the Russian Czar.

The father spoke to her:

"Listen, my daughter, when you go,
If the husband does not get wood,
You can burn the scythe, rakes,
Axe handles, skis, ski poles,
Gun handles. Burn them all as firewood,
If the husband does not get wood."

Chapter Three

"Cuckoo there, little cuckoo,
Call away, sandy-breasted,
Call out evenings, call out mornings,
Even in the mid-day calling,
To rejoice the skies above me,
For the cheering of my woodlands,
For the richness of my shores
And the good life all about me!"

Kalevala, Runo 2

When they returned from Oulanka, Matt went back to the Helsinki shipyards and Taisto started on his farm—clearing trees and digging ditches. Some of this drainage work had been done by those before him, and Taisto thought with this headstart he could make it, even if all around him thousands of young people were leaving for America. Lempi said to live with her until a house could be built, but throughout the summer Taisto was too busy on the land to even think of a house. The mosquitoes ate him alive in the ditches and though he did manage to plant a few acres of rye, the frost came early. Maybe he couldn't make it farming. He thought maybe he should go with Matt next spring to America. But he wouldn't tell Senja yet—not until after the baby came.

The morning after Christmas Senja said that the time had come. Taisto warmed the sauna and in she went. She stripped, and crawled up on the bench. Lempi came in and out, filling the water barrel, and scrubbing and sweeping in the changing room that connected to the sauna, setting out clean towels and bedding.

Senja laboured on the high bench, sometimes sitting, sometimes lying on her back, then on her side. Every once in a while, with a wooden dipper, she threw a little water on the stones. She didn't want it too hot as too much heat might sap her strength.

Senja's pains became sharper, more intense, and she climbed down from the bench. She stood on the floor, her legs parted and bent, and her hands reached up and grabbed the foot rail. She grunted, concentrating, urging her working body. She filled the dipper with water and poured it on her shoulders. Lempi came into the room, humming, and sprinkled water from a birch twig *vasta* on the stones. The sauna filled with the *vasta's* medicinal aroma.

Senja emitted a soft, yet piercing wail, and she bent lower, grunting harder. Lempi worked her hands down Senja's back, humming over and over, kneading Senja's flesh.

Senja grasped hard at the footrail, gave one sudden lunge, and there it came.

For three days the mother and baby stayed in the sauna.

While Senja slept, nursed the baby, and slept some more, Lempi was back and forth from the house, bringing food, washing out the sauna, and changing the bedding.

On the third day Senja brought the baby to the house. She walked across the floor towards Taisto who was carving a piece of birch beside the fire. He rose to his feet, setting his knife and carving down. She placed the child in his arms and he looked at it. Taisto nodded, and, without smiling, held the child away from his body, lifting it up and down, weighing it with his hands. He unwrapped it and checked the fingers and toes.

"He is a good baby, ya." Taisto smiled, and held the baby high before him. "Ya that is a 'hero', this baby." Taisto's jaw jutted to one side, and, looking at the two women, he strutted about the room. "Ya, that is what we will name him. We will name him a hero. We will name him 'Urho!'"

A month later Taisto made up his mind. He would go to

America. He kicked snow from his boots and entered the cottage. Sitting at the table he tapped his fingers slowly, and then dug his nails into the wood and scratched. Taisto had been thinking about emigrating, but he hadn't said anything to Senja. He'd been proud of himself, getting enough land cleared to plant the rye. But then the frost—all that work for nothing. The fish pedlar had swindled him—that's for sure, and that crook could have the land back before he got another *penni* out of Taisto. The stub of a lighted splinter on the wall snuffed out and he replaced it. At the fireplace Lempi worked her loom, weaving a rug she was going to send to her brother, Tenho, if she could find the money for posting. Senja rocked in Lempi's chair, singing quietly to the nursing baby.

Taisto breathed deeply, and scratched his nails again and again into the soft wood of the table. Then he laid his fingers flat, rose from his bench, and gazed towards Lempi. He tried to make out the colours in the rug, but failing to see in the darkness, he walked to the loom. She makes it like the rainbow, he thought, and he wondered if in America he could make a loom for Senja. In April he would go to work for two months in the shipyard in Helsinki with Matt Inhonen. He could earn enough for passage to America.

He went to Senja, pulled a bench up close, and faced her. He touched the baby, felt its tiny mouth moving on Senja's breast. Then he drew his hand away. "I have decided. I will go to America," he said.

"Yes," Senja said, quietly.

"When April comes I go to Helsinki to earn money. Matt Inhonen still is there. He and I will go to America."

"Yes." She patted the baby on the back, burping him.

Taisto's stern look changed into a smile, and Senja looked happily at him, grabbed his hand, and squeezed. He sat up straight on his bench. It wouldn't be long—he could make money in America, and send for them. There would be opportunity for them and his son. He stood, walked over to the door, opened it and ran out into the snow, up to his knees. He ran in circles.

"Close the door," Lempi shouted. "What is the matter with your head? Do you want to bring the cold for the baby?" Senja laughed. "Do we go crazy in the winter?"

"Voi! Voi!" Lempi said, "that is a Finn—grouchy like a bear all winter, and all of the sudden crazy."

Lempi wondered. What will she and Senja do? What will it be like when Taisto leaves for America? Senja can stay as long as she wishes—how can a mother take a baby to the other end of the earth? Lempi stared at her carvings above the door, the cuckoo bird, and the weasel. She tightened the rug on the loom. Always it is the young men who leave. Ya, Senja and I will go to Helsinki before the ship sails, go to watch Taisto leave. Maybe we can have photographs taken, have a likeness of Taisto for us to keep. Who knows when we see him again. Maybe I should send one to Tenho in America, write to him that Taisto is coming.

Chapter Four

Ukko, lord of heaven above,
Rubbed his palms, then pressed them down
Both together on his left knee.
This gave birth to three young maidens,
All of them creation's daughters,
Mothers to the ore of iron,
Begetters of the blue-bite metal.
Lightly swaying went the maidens,
Walked the virgins on a cloud rim,
With their full breasts overbrimming
As their nipples ached for milking.
Sprayed their milk upon the earth,
Milked their teats most copiously—
Milk on highland, milk on lowland
Milk upon the quiet waters.

Kalevala, Runo 9

Taisto stood alongside Matt Inhonen leaning on the deck
railing of the big ship. It was the second day out, and the
excitement of the voyage had worn thin for him. He thought of
Senja and felt guilty, wishing it was she and not Matti beside
him. Instead she had to stay behind, waiting for another baby.
Senja will have two little ones to care for and no father to help.

He gazed out at the roll of the sea. How long would it
be before Senja could join him? Would he get rich in America?

Matt spoke. "Are you down in the dumps, Taisto? You
hang your head like you are ready to fall into the sea. What's
the matter? You miss your wife? Don't worry, she is a good
wife. She will wait—not like some."

Taisto spit into the water.

"Ya," Matt said. "You seem angry. You have heard the shipyard gossip?"

"No, what gossip?"

"Didn't you hear? A man went to America to work in the iron mines. He left the shipyards to pick gold coins off American streets—left his wife and son in Finland." From his haversack, Matt pulled out a bread roll. He dropped pieces over the rail, and watched a gull swoop to catch the bread before it hit the water.

"Ya," Taisto said, "gold coins. Like all of us, it is easy to dream."

Taisto worshipped Matt, always so smart, always thinking, always sure of himself. He seemed to know the reasons people did what they did, and Taisto wished he could be a little bit like that. He gazed down at the water, and sucked the last smoke from his pipe. He tapped the hardwood bowl against the iron railing, and ashes fell, spreading in the salt breeze. For a moment he held the warm pipe bowl close to his nose. He took a knife from his boot-top and scraped inside the bowl, scraping hard peelings of blackish residue into the palm of his hand as he had seen old men do in the north, and like the old men, he put the scrapings inside his lower lip.

"So what's the gossip? This man, did he make his fortune?"

"After three years he came back to Helsinki, and there he saw his wife...," Matt held his hand out in front of his stomach, "big, she was big as a haystack."

"Three years he was gone?" Taisto asked. "What did he do to her?"

"Nothing to her—he took his fourteen-year-old son and went back to America."

Matt threw another scrap of bread overboard. A gull squawked, swooped, and missed, and the bread hit the water. Another gull snatched the morsel up. Matt continued. "When the ship arrived in the New York harbour, the boy could not find his father."

"Jumped overboard?" Taisto guessed.

"How did you know?"

"That's what a Finn would do," Taisto said. "There are many such stories." He remembered Lempi's *Kalevala*, the story of *Aino*, and how she sank beneath the water's surface. "Remember mother's singing about *Väinämöinen*? How the women rejected him? Twelve different women! *Aino* denied *Väinämöinen* by drowning herself in the lake."

For several minutes Matt said nothing, and then he spoke. "It is not of any benefit for a socialist to waste his brains on fairy tales," he said. "You know, Taisto, those who rule have done so by feeding us with those myths. The working man must look forward, not back."

They heard loud cheers from a crowd on deck at the far end of the ship, and ran to see what was happening.

All were young men, Finns on one side of a big circle, and Swedes on the other. In the centre, with his shirt off and a broom-stick in his hand, a tall Swede with a missing front tooth flexed his muscles, grinned to the cheering group of countrymen and jeered at the Finns. A man sat on the deck, looking at the broomstick and rubbing his hands. He rose to his feet and stumbled, half-raised one hand, more to steady himself than anything else, and moved into the crowd of Finns.

"No more takers?" the big Swede said. His supporters laughed.

The Finns mumbled.

"Is there nobody else?" he said.

A few seconds passed, then Matt Inhonen entered the circle, took off his shirt and paced seven long steps to face the grinning Swede. Matt shrugged. Taisto watched from the circle. What does he think, this big ape? Does he think only a Swede can win at the game of twisting the broomstick? Wait till he tries Matt.

A seagull squawked from the railing, flew to perch on a ventilator stack rising from the lower deck, then flew back to the railing where it squawked again. The Swede's handler stood between the contestants.

"Only one knee has to touch," the handler said. "One

knee on the deck, and that's it. You don't have to put a man down on both knees."

Across from the handler, a little Finn with pointed shoes held a can of pine tar. The handler grabbed the can and passed it to Matt. "For your hands," he said.

The contest began. For a long time both men stood poised, unmoving, with the broomstick above their heads. Beads of sweat popped on their foreheads and their muscles bulged and gleamed. From the gap in his teeth, saliva trickled down the Swede's chin. The seagull squawked, flying back and forth from the railing to the ventilator. Several times the Swede lunged, trying to force Matt down, but the Finn remained fixed in his position, giving nothing, taking nothing.

The Swede's grin had long since changed to a frown. He turned to his handler, then to Matt, then back at his handler. When the Swede looked away the second time, Matt lunged and twisted down on the handle.

Taisto was surprised when the man didn't go down, but instead the Swede simply raised his fingers, turned his palms up and looked at them. Then Taisto saw the blood, and the skin from the Swede's hands stuck to the tar on the broomstick. The crowd was silent and still, except for the little Finn with the pointed shoes, who danced with an imaginary broomstick held before him, once in a while giving it a quick twist.

New York harbour, Ellis Island, Statue of Liberty, streets full of rushing people—Taisto laughed to himself. Is this the new land where streets are paved with gold? "Ya," He rubbed the sole of his boot on the wooden sidewalk. "I don't see the gold. Maybe we are too late."

"Maybe there is gold in Michigan," Matt said.

Taisto sensed a feeling of oneness with all the young people milling about, even the Swedes, most of them poor like himself, coming off ships, hurrying to board trains. Should he believe what they had preached at the workers' club meetings in Helsinki, the politics of the Social Democrats? Would their politics come to fruit in this new land? Matt believed it would.

Matt said that the minds of the young people would be freed from the old rules of their fathers and the landlords. Taisto wondered, is it really true, this Statue of Liberty—does the Mother welcomes us?

By train they went to Hancock, Michigan. Lempi had told Taisto that her brother, Tenho Maki, was at Hancock. But when they arrived there, and asked about for a Laestadian pastor by that name, a Finn at the railway station, who was arguing with the agent at the wicket about the price of a ticket to Duluth, said he had never heard of a Tenho Maki. "Ya, but there is a Laestadian pastor," he said. "I will take you. He lives beside the barber shop."

Ten minutes later they were sitting at the pastor's table, drinking coffee. "Ya, I know Maki," the pastor said. "He is a good friend—one of God's children who brought the Faith to Hancock many years ago from Finland."

"Where is he now?" Matt asked.

"Gone to farm in Minnesota—married a widow. The husband was killed in the mine just last year. She had six children, one more coming."

"Ya, he will need a farm," Matt said. "Is it far to this farm?"

"By train north and west through the Iron Range, maybe a day, then south, you have to walk...."

"Ya, the Iron Range," Taisto said. "That is the mining."

"Oh, ya," the pastor said. "Here at Hancock it is only the copper. There it is the iron, Vermillion Range, Mesabi Range. Many from here have gone—to Duluth. At Duluth the U.S. Steel Companies hire the men, many Finns."

At the railway station in Duluth a man with a big ledger book took Matt and Taisto's names and directed them to a boat taking men to Two Harbours on the big lake's west shore. At Two Harbours they watched the ore train unload at the Soudan Mine docks and rode back on the empty train to the mine.

From out of the thick forest of pine and spruce trees the

train rolled into the mine site at the end of a sixty-mile ride from the docks. It was raining when they arrived at the Soudan Mine. They heard squeals above the clankings of the empty ore cars, above the scream of the braked wheels—frightening squeals that pierced the comforting huffs and puffs of the train engine. Matt and Taisto joined a commotion of shouting, laughing, and cursing men surrounding a mule tied to a heavy post. The mule tugged at its tether, brayed its awful sounds as a husky workman pulled on a rope slung over the mule's back and tied to its right front foot. The mule was on three legs.

"He can't kick now," said one of a dozen wet spectators.

"Those mules aren't stupid like us Finns," another man said. "To get us down the shaft, the Company doesn't have to put us in a strait jacket."

"What's the difference?" said the miner who was pulling the mule's rope. "Wet down there—wet up here."

"Ya," said a miner with a bushy moustache that curled up the sides of his cheeks. He straightened his hunched shoulders, pulled at the peak of his cap, and addressed himself to all who could hear. "All us miners need is to have as much sense as a mule. When a mule is overloaded, he doesn't pray to God for relief. He just kicks like hell."

Across from them a clean-shaven man in a bowler hat, double-breasted suit, and polished oxfords that he wiped now and then with a rag, pointed his finger at the struggling mule. He spoke in English to the four workmen applying the ropes and straps. The workmen looked only at the mule, and at each other. They worked slowly, tugging at a leather strap, clipping a snap on a ring, studying the harness to make sure that there would be no mistake in the binding of this mule. Each man did his own job in silence, working with the precision of the gears in a clock. Now and then one of them uttered a muffled word or two in Finn.

Taisto looked up at the towering cone of wet timbers housing the shaft down into the mine, at the steel cables running from the tower to the engine house. He saw that the four men were tying the mule in order to get it down the shaft. They girded a belly strap around the animal's middle, secured a canvas strapping around its rump and across the chest. They put a hood over the mule's head and iron rings on its back feet. The left front foot was tied, and the mule dropped to its knees. With ropes joining the rings on the back feet to rings on the belly strap, the workmen pulled the hind legs forward and its rump went down. They wrapped the mule as if it were an Egyptian mummy, and rolled it onto a cart. They took it to the cage, sat it up straight like a bowling pin, and down they went into the mine.

The man with the polished shoes said something in English to Matt and Taisto which they could not understand.

The miner with the bushy moustache translated—"He wants to know if you have any experience working with heavy timbers."

"Ya," Matt said, "in the shipyards."

"He says to go to that building. The clerk there will make your tags for you." He showed him the brass token pinned to his overalls—*Soudan Mines,* then a number, and the man's name. "There was a big explosion in #7 tunnel yesterday. Using candles to warm the dynamite to get it to the blasting temperature. Two men killed. None of us will go to clean out that tunnel."

"Are you striking?" Matt asked.

"No, but we boycott that tunnel for those killed. I suppose it's okay for you new guys to go down. There's talk in town, though, about forming a union, so maybe you can come sometime to the Finn Hall? Say, you are newcomers to America. Why don't I buy you a drink tonight. There is a tavern on the main street, you will see it—The Waverly House. Suppose I meet you there? Ten o'clock."

Matt and Taisto had to walk around a seated group of non-Finns to reach the small table in the corner where the moustached miner sat. The miner ordered beer, and the three men sat drinking in silence, watching other men shaking water from their caps as they entered from the street. At the bar, a woman with bright lipstick and flaming red hair wound in coils around the top of her head talked with an elderly miner in bib overalls. He set his lunch bucket on the counter and fiddled with the snaps, opening and closing the lid. Over a period of ten minutes, the old man gulped three shot glasses of whiskey. The woman talked, he listened and nodded several times. The bartender was about to fill the old man's glass again, when the woman smiled and shook her head, then pushed her own glass forward to be filled.

Back at the crowded table near the entrance, the commotion increased. One of the noise-makers got to his feet.

"Hey, ya stinkin' Mongolians!" he said, waving his whiskey glass, pointing at the Finns.

"Should I translate?" the moustached miner said to Matt and Taisto.

The man wobbled back and forth on his feet, whiskey spilling on his hand. He fell against the table. His companions reached for their glasses and stopped his fall at the same time.

"Why don't you go back to Finland?" the man went on. His friends hooted and stood him back up on his feet. "Why don't we get the blessed St. Patrick to drive these bastards out of here, and back to where they came from—like the Holy Patron Saint did with the snakes—God bless him." He turned to his companions, and they roared all the more with laughter. "What is this bullshit about a strike?" he yelled. As he drank, slobber and whiskey trickled down his chin.

"Ya, that is a noisy fellow," Matt said. "What does he say?"

"He says," the miner translated, "we are not welcome here."

The drunk stumbled across the room, up to a table of Finns, and hovered over a little man seated on a low stool.

"Where did you get those curly little boots?" he said. "Ya look like a bleedin' Leprechaun."

The little Finn smiled nervously. The Irishman grabbed the whiskey bottle from the table and threw it across the room, smashing it against the wall a foot above Taisto's head. The men at the little Finn's table all began talking at once.

"Quit that foreign gibberish," the Irishman yelled.

Taisto and the moustached man stood up, but Matt grabbed both of them by the arm and sat them down. At the other table the little Finn reached into his boot top for his knife. From every Finnish table came the whisper, *puukko, puukko*. He goes for his knife!

The little Finn's arm flashed, and the Irishman fell back, his open hand grabbing at the gash on his face. The Irishman held his shaking glass with both hands in front of him, and the whiskey spilled, mixing with the blood running down the sides of the glass.

His companions rose from their table, smashed their whiskey glasses, and started for the little Finn. Then from the Finnish tables came the whispers, *puukko, puukko, puukko*, and the miners reached into their boots for their knives. The Irishmen stopped, and holding up their drunken companion, backed towards the door, and out to the wet sidewalk.

"We'll get you foreign bastards," one of them called.

If there is a devil, he is in this hole, Taisto thought. Do we dig all the way to hell? He dreaded going down the main shaft, but the tunnels were worse. At least there was an electric light in the shaft. The tunnel to the ore body was a different story. The tunnel was damp, it was cold, and black, as black as *Väinämöinen's* underworld journey through *Tuonela*, through the death-dark river of *Tuoni*, through the caverns of the dead. What possessed a man to put three candles in his pocket, a fourth spiked to his helmet, and to spend ten hours drilling holes into solid rock in a cold and black cave two hundred feet under the ground? At least at the shipyard he could see the sky.

It was two weeks after the tavern incident. In the morning they had dynamited and shovelled ore down the chute to the Irish trammers in the tunnel below them. After lunch they pried out loose rock from the walls and roof to make preparation for more shoring. They had heard a clunk, then the explosion. Someone had thrown a stick of dynamite into their tunnel. Rock falling. Timbers. Dust.

"Hey! The roof!" Matt yelled. "Watch out!" Taisto tasted dust, stumbled across loose rock, and bumped against the tunnel wall. He couldn't see anything. "Where are you, Matti? Are you alright?"

"Ya, over here! Over here! There's no damn light. Son of a bitch!" Matti yelled. "Dynamite! Son of a bitch Irish. He tried to kill us!"

On his knees, Taisto groped with his hands, felt the fallen rock, and reached out for his friend. Then he heard him yell.

"Matches, you have matches, Taisto?"

"Wait. Ya. The pocket of my overalls. I have two matches left."

"Don't light yet! Wait! The candles, can we find the candles?"

Taisto swept his palms carefully along the floor. They had lighted their last two candles, and had spiked them into the tunnel wall just minutes before the ceiling fell. Where were they? He spread his fingers, combing through the rubble. There was so much, so many pieces of rock. How could he find a candle?

"Where are you?" Matt asked. "Where are you?"

"Over here, Matti. Can I light one match?"

"What do you think? Wait!" Matt said.

Taisto crawled back and forth, sideways, going nowhere over the rubble on the tunnel floor.

"Damn!" Matt yelled.

Taisto stopped moving, and he tried to sense where things were. Why not light a match? At least he'd find Matt. "Can I light a match, Matti?"

"Okay, Taisto, light the match."

Before he did he saw light appear far along in the tunnel, coming towards them. Men had come looking. Taisto could hear their shouts.

Chapter Five

"Do not, child of mother born,
Do not fret about what's coming.
You won't be in a worse position,
Rather in a better station
There beside your plowman husband,
Under the cloak of furrow-maker;
On the breast of your breadwinner
In the arms of your fish-catcher;
In the sweat of your elk-skier,
With the bear-killer in the sauna.

Kalevala, Runo 22

To hell with the mines. They will go to Tenho Maki's farm—
they would find him. He is in Menahga—Matti asked at the
Soudan church. They would go right away and have the whole
summer at Menahga to find work on the farms. Anything was
better than an iron mine.

Menahga was more than one hundred and fifty miles
southwest of Soudan. They were told to take the Duluth,
Missabi, and Northern Railway across the Mesabi Iron Range
through the towns of Virginia, Mountain Iron, Hibbing, and
Nashwauk. From Nashwauk they could walk to Menahga in a
few days.

Matt and Taisto came through the trees, on a footpath, into
Tenho's yard. They saw a young woman run from the sauna to
the house, carrying a child wrapped in a towel. In no time at all,
a man of middle years, his head tilted slightly to the side, came
off the veranda. His hair was pure white, and it hung thinly
across his forehead. His skin was as finely textured as his hair,

and in places his thin cheeks showed pink blotches. Though wrinkles appeared around his eyes, the eyes themselves, the lightest of blues, were full of life. They gleamed. He approached and fixed his eyes on Taisto, squinted, turned his head more to the side, frowned, and slowly a smile grew. He yelled over his shoulder, "Maria, Maria, there is company," and the excitement in his eyes was proof that his road-weary guests were welcome.

"I know one of you," he said.

"How could that be?" Taisto asked.

"You are Taisto, Lempi's son."

Matt walked over to the woodpile by the sauna. He picked up the axe and felt its edge, and then turned his attention back to the conversation.

Taisto knew by now that he was talking to Tenho Maki.

"How do you know that I am Taisto?"

"I can tell by the family look," Tenho said.

Taisto shook his head. "I was but a baby when you left Finland, Tenho. That was twenty years ago."

"No, no," Tenho laughed. "I cannot recognize you from a baby. No—I have a letter from Lempi, and she has sent a likeness. I recognize you from your photograph."

He laughed again, and shook Taisto's hand. "You come in time for Saturday afternoon sauna."

"I am Matt Inhonen," Matt said, setting the axe down, and walking forward, he extended his hand to Tenho. "Taisto is a friend of mine. We have come from Finland together."

"Ya, Lempi has said in the letter about a Matti coming with Taisto. You are in the photograph."

Children began appearing from different places. A boy in a yellow shirt watched them from behind the woodpile. At the well an older boy wearing a cap pumped water and carried it to the sauna. Three bare-footed girls in white smocks peeked from one side of the house, and from the other side came an older woman carrying a little boy.

"Maria, before you take Fred to the sauna, come and meet my sister's boy from Finland. This is Taisto, and his friend, Matt Inhonen."

Tenho's wife turned and smiled shyly. She eyed the girls by the house and the boy at the woodpile, cautioning them with her gaze not to be overly forward. Maria's black hair was combed back and gathered into a bun at the back of her head, exposing a broad forehead and squared cheek-bones. She had darker skin than her husband, muscular hands, and her body from the broad shoulders down to the hips amply filled her print dress.

The young woman Matt and Taisto had seen when they first came into the yard appeared on the veranda. On her skirted hip she was holding the child she had carried from the sauna, a baby girl. She wore her hair loose, and her free hand played with a strand of it, rubbing the tips against her chin. Tenho noticed the men watching her.

"Ya, Taisto. You must remember Ruth. My daughter. All the rest are Maria's children. The baby girl began to cry and Ruth bounced it gently on her hip, keeping her eyes on the gathering in the front yard. She had her father's eyes, gleaming and the lightest of blue, and so alive that the eyes drew all the attention.

Tenho led his guests into the house to the round kitchen table that was already set with a plate of prune tarts and doughnuts. The room was filled with the smell of coffee simmering on the stove, put there to boil by Maria at the first sight of visitors.

"How is Lempi?" Tenho said, filling cups with coffee. "Do you think Lempi will ever come to America?"

Tenho reached in the cupboard for the lumps of hard sugar the men favoured with coffee. He put a lump in his mouth, spilled the hot coffee from his cup into his saucer, and drank from the saucer. Matt and Taisto did the same.

Taisto had never given much thought to his mother's coming to America. Maybe she would come with Senja, but he couldn't imagine Lempi wanting to leave Finland to come here. Where would she fit? She was thirty-seven years old. Surely it is only the young ones who come, Taisto thought, and that is because they have to—there is nothing for them in Finland. But Lempi? Isn't Finland everything to her? He was eager only for Senja. It wouldn't be long until the new baby. I wonder if Urho has teeth. He is probably crawling all over the place. It is good that Senja has Mother with her.

"Ya," Taisto said, "I don't know if Mother would come. Did she say anything in her letter?"

Before Tenho could answer, Ruth descended from upstairs with a stack of clean towels cradled on her arm, and the men turned their heads to her. She blushed, quickened her step, set the towels on the cupboard and shyly glanced to the kitchen table, indicating to the guests that these were their bath towels. Then she turned her head away, her dark hair sweeping her shoulder, and quickly left the room.

"Ya," Tenho said, "I think Maria has bathed the children. We will finish our coffee, and then we go to sauna."

"Ya," Matt said, "we can talk some more in there."

Tenho was proud of his modern bath-house. In the old smoke saunas the men had to bathe first. The rocks would be red hot and the room filled with smoke. One dipper of water and the blast of hot steam would clear the air. Only a man could take it, a Finn. The women had to wait for the gentle steam that came once the rocks had lost their intense heat. But his new sauna had a chimney, and Maria could take the baby in while the rocks were still warming, and not be choked up with smoke.

Ya, Tenho thought, it is hot now. I wonder how much steam these boys from Finland can handle? I wonder if they are as tough as I used to be?

"Pour the steam, ya," Taisto said, rubbing his palms against his ribs. "Pour the steam." They all three sat on the high bench, Taisto in the middle, and Tenho, with the bucket and dipper, above the sauna stove.

Each time Tenho threw a dipper of water on the rocks, Taisto could feel the hot steam on the bottoms of his feet, and along his back muscles below the rib cage. Beads of sweat collected on his arms and shoulders, and when he rubbed his biceps with his fingers, dirt and skin rolled into tiny balls.

"Not enough fire," Tenho said, crawling off the bench. He loaded the stove with an armful of freshly cut kindling, and opened the draft.

Taisto heard the sudden roar of the fire. Tenho has a good sauna, he thought, and he scooped water with his hands from a large basin, splashing it on his face and hair. The steam bit into the skin around his lips, his ears, his fingers and toes, and along his calves.

Matt got down off the bench.

"Too much steam?" Tenho asked, and threw another dipper, then waved his arms fanning the hot air. Taisto dunked his head in the basin and splashed

"No," Matt said. "I need my knife." He opened the door to the change room, got his knife, and climbed back up on the bench. He propped his feet on a rail, and began paring his toe-nails.

Tenho threw steam for several minutes until his bucket was empty. He then reached down into a pail of water and pulled out a bundle of birch tree branches. Ya, just like in Finland, Taisto thought. What is a sauna without a good whipping across the back with a *vasta*? Who can take the most steam and show that it is nothing? Be a man and swat yourself across the back. Ya, let Matti fight the old man. Taisto got off the bench and pointed to his chest. "Oh, ya, the *vasta*. No, I think I have had enough steam," and having acknowledged his defeat, he went outside to dry off in the cool air.

Over the hot stones, Tenho shook the wet birch leaves and the sauna filled with the medicinal smell of birch. Matt, following Tenho's example, reached for his own *vasta,* and filling the sauna with hot and aromatic steam, swatted himself across the back and legs repeatedly. His skin turned even redder, and he could feel its tingle—half pain, half pleasure. Matt and Tenho heated their *vastas* once again and swatted each other. For five minutes they continued until Matt could barely breathe. The men faced each other, each with *vasta* raised, and for a moment, held them in that pose. Is this never going to end, Matt thought? Then Tenho set his *vasta* on the bench, picked up the basin of water, and dumped it on his head. He looked at Matt, still holding his *vasta* as if to strike, and Tenho began laughing. Matt set his *vasta* down, staring at Tenho who continued laughing, and then he laughed too.

"I guess it is a draw," Tenho said, and he got down from the bench, filled the basin from the barrel on the floor, and doused himself again.

On the day they arrived, Matt had wondered whose baby it was that Ruth Maki carried on her hip, and when he found out later that it was Maria's youngest, a little girl named Eva, he was relieved, and not at all displeased to spend the summer grubbing stumps on Tenho's farm. The arrangement was especially helpful for Tenho because much of his summer was taken up with missionary work among the pockets of Laestadian congregations throughout Minnesota, Wisconsin, and northern Michigan.

Matt and Tenho rarely discussed politics, though Tenho was fully aware of the Marxist wave of social democracy underway in Finland, and its equally alarming cancer-like spread among Finns across the Mesabi. Socialism stuck to Finns like hot grease to skin. He prayed that Matt would seek God's saving grace, but he doubted that that would happen.

Matt liked Tenho, and tried his best to develop a relationship with the Makis that avoided both politics and religion. He knew how difficult the task would be because religion was Tenho's reason for being, and politics was his own.

One evening, late in the fall, when Tenho and Maria were away at Services in Cokato, Ruth sent Matt and Taisto to Menahga with the cream and eggs.

On their return, they could see the light through the trees.

"Do you see?" Matt said. "Ahead of us, look, through the leaves. It could be at the farmhouse."

"That's a fire!" Taisto yelled. Both men raced along

the footpath. "That's fire! Matti! The house is on fire!"

They ran into the yard, and Ruth was standing by the veranda, her hands clenched and raised above her head. She screamed at them. "Upstairs! Upstairs!"

Matt looked in a window on the veranda, shook his head, and raced to the sauna. He jumped into the water-barrel and submerged himself, then ran back to the veranda. "Taisto!" he yelled, "look after Ruth!" He disappeared into the house.

"I was in the barn!" she yelled, "Taisto! I was in the barn! The girls must have been playing with the lamp! When I came to the house, the stairs were burning. I couldn't get to them."

Taisto grabbed her, but she fought him off, screamed, pulled her hair, and shook her clenched hands over her head.

Matt appeared on the veranda, a child on each arm, and fire and smoke belching out the open door. He stumbled off the veranda away from the burning house and towards Ruth.

"I found only two." He coughed, almost collapsing to the ground, his arms wide at his sides, holding the babies. Both children were crying, choking with smoke.

He handed little Fred to Taisto, and Ruth took the girl. For a moment she gazed at the fire and then turned at Matt.

Ruth's face changed, growing stranger and stranger. "Only two?" she said. Her eyes, usually so full of life, now appeared to contain no life at all. The only light that came from them was the light of the fire. She had stopped screaming when Matt came out of the house, but now there was no movement in her face at all. Then slowly, a tremble touched her lip, and then a twitch along her chin. She stumbled, and her arms shook. Taisto took the baby from her. More and more her face trembled, straining, and she made high-pitched choking sounds, her hands clutching at her throat and cheeks. Matt went to her, and Taisto stepped back with the babies in his arms.

Her choking sounds changed to a gush of loud keening wails, and she pounded her fists on Matt's chest. She pounded till her knees buckled out from under her, and Matt had to keep her from falling. Leaning away from him, with both hands pulling at his shirt, she swung her head, back and forth, her hair trailing, back and forth. Then with her fists hanging on to his shirt, she rested her head on his shoulder, and her cries softened. He held her like that until neighbours began to arrive.

At midnight Taisto located the station agent and got him to send a telegraph to Cokato, to Tenho and Maria. While they waited, Taisto wished more than anything else that his mother was with him. She would know what to do: how to comfort Ruth, what to do with the five bodies, what to tell Tenho. Lempi would know how to be with Maria, and take some of her grief. But his mother was in Finland, and he'd have to do as best he could.

But it wasn't only Taisto's worry. By the time Tenho and Maria arrived the following afternoon, scores of neighbours and Laestadian believers had made all the arrangements. Their closest believing neighbour simply took the family into his home. In a week's time a work-bee had constructed a new log house with a kitchen, sitting room, two bedrooms on the ground floor, and a sleeping loft upstairs.

By the following spring Tenho Maki had decided to move.

He had made the same decision twenty years earlier when his first wife and son drowned. No matter how much he believed that these earthly matters could be put away by faith, staying in Menahga would always remind him of the horrible burning death of Maria's five children. And he saw what it was doing to Maria. She had aged at least five years, and had lost interest in everything. She didn't want to visit, had quit weaving, and left most of the care of tiny Eva and Fred to his daughter Ruth. Tenho decided to move far away, but he wasn't sure where to go until he had talked it over with Matt.

Matt showed Tenho an advertisement in *Työmies*, listing land opening for homesteads in Canada. Tenho called *Työmies* 'that socialist rag from Duluth', but still he considered the land offer too good to pass up. And so Tenho Maki, and Matt Inhonen agreed to emigrate again, this time to Saskatchewan,

Canada. Taisto disagreed. He wanted to earn some money so Senja could join him in America. He would go to the big open-pit mine at Hibbing.

Tenho knew that there was a matter to be settled before the move to Canada could be made. His daughter was in love with an unbeliever. In their duty as believing parents, he and Maria had counselled her on the dangers of the flesh. By keeping company with an unbeliever Ruth was succumbing to the Devil.

On the Sunday after Easter, in the morning, Matt and Ruth entered the Maki sitting room. Tenho sat upright on a wooden chair, stiffly, his eyes focused on the rain outside the window, and Maria rocked beside him, rubbing her hands, her head bent downward.

Matt and Ruth sat on a rug-covered bench, facing them. No one spoke for a long time. Matt noticed Maria's hands, how she rubbed them. Water droplets trickled down the window. Rain pattered on the roof and he could hear a robin chirping.

Tenho's hands pressed to his knees, his head shook and his blue eyes watered as he looked away from the window to Ruth.

"Tenho," Matt said. His fingers gripped the bench. He did not look at Ruth, but only at Tenho's shaking head. "Ruth and I want to marry."

Tenho stared at Matt only for a moment, then spoke to Ruth.

"Do you know what you are doing?"

Matt sensed in Ruth the same tightness she had shown the night of the fire. She inched away from him on the bench, and Maria glanced up at her. He could barely hear Ruth's words.

"I love him," she said. The words seemed to crack, as if she were choking, and her body shook. Tears spilled from her eyes, and her fingers, clawing at her cheeks, were wet.

"You are a believer, Ruth."

Matt gripped the bench harder—he wanted to hold her,

to assure her, yet all the while he had no doubts about what she would choose.

"I am a believer but I love Matt, too," she said.

Tenho's gaze returned to the window, and he nodded slightly, several times.

"Will you marry us, Tenho?" Matt asked.

"Yes," Tenho said.

Ruth wiped the tears from her eyes. "I will keep the Faith," she said.

Chapter Six

Then Kullervo Kalervoson,
Old man's son in blue stockings,
Placed the hilt upon the ground,
Pressed the haft against the heath;

Kalevala, Runo 36

Senja received Taisto's letter on St. John's Day, the day of the Mid-summer festivals—the day of the summer solstice, when the sky in Kuusamo is light around the clock. Lempi had brought the letter home from the village. She climbed out of her little boat and tied it to a birch tree growing between two rotting stumps. This reminded her of the outing with Taisto the winter before last. She hurried up the footpath. In the little meadow beside her cottage she saw Senja amid the haystacks. What a worker, that Senja. In the morning the hay poles stood like barren crosses. Now they were full.

"Senja! Senja!" Lempi waved the letter over her head. "Another letter from Taisto, Senja!"

"What is it?" Senja put a finger to her lips then pointed to the house. "The children are sleeping."

"A letter from Taisto. Read it and then tell me what he says."

The two women sat on a bench against the cottage wall facing the sun. Senja examined the envelope. The postmark was April 21, 1905. More than two months getting here! She opened the envelope carefully, and carefully unfolded the letter. She read silently, page after page, and only then did she speak, reading bits to Lempi. "Taisto agrees to name the baby, Sirkku. He is happy to know that you thought of it, Lempi. A nice name for a girl, he says. He says his cousin Ruth has married Matt Inhonen and they are moving to Canada, along with your brother Tenho. Taisto is mining at Hibbing, Minnesota. There are many Finns. He says he goes sometimes to dances at the workers' hall, just to watch, and that he misses me dearly." Senja wrapped her arms across her breasts, closed her eyes, and rocked from side to side.

"Dances!" Lempi said. "Hasn't Taisto got anything better to do?" She could see how Senja was lost in her thoughts, humming to herself, pretending to dance with Taisto in America. Ya, Senja will dance in this America. It is not good for the young to go there, but they go just the same. May God protect them in that Devil's Land. Lempi walked back down to the boat for the few supplies she brought from the village. She would let Senja be by herself to enjoy her letter.

Another letter came in the fall, but not from Taisto. It was from Haapajarvi.... Haapajarvi? Lempi wondered. Is that not the village near the old Nordholm hunting lodge? It can't be—that is too long ago, and I am getting old. I'm thirty-nine. Surely that Olovi Nordholm doesn't remember—doesn't keep an interest in....*Voi! Voi!* How stupid of me to think of that man.

But she couldn't help thinking it was the same hunting lodge. She could feel her flesh break into a cold sweat. But the letter was addressed to Senja, she thought.

"It's from Otto! My brother!" Senja said. "He has a job at a hunting lodge. All the gentry will be away during the holidays, and he invites us to spend New Year's with him. That would be fun, yes, Lempi?"

Otto Jukola, proud to be driving the horses of the *Jääkari* cavalry, proud to be serving the cause of Finland, proud to be led by the great Mannerhein, and above all, proud to fight against Russian domination, looked back at his two female passengers and the two bundled toddlers. He whipped the horses and the sleigh seemed to fly across the snow.

"See!" Otto said, as the sleigh broke into the wide clearing, "the big lodge. We are building four more cabins for

Jääkari recruits. Everyone has gone home for the holiday, and then some will be sent to Germany for more training."

The clearing was as Lempi remembered it, except for the newly added barracks and stables. The two spruce trees at the front entrance had grown enormously, but of course why not? Twenty-five years is a long time for growing. She led Urho by the hand and followed Senja who was carrying Sirkku into the building.

The couch had been replaced by another done in brown leather with gold studding, but it was draped with the same old fur wrap. Lempi stroked the smooth pile of the reindeer fur and sat on the couch, helping Urho with his coat. Senja took some of Sirkku's winter wrappings off and let her walk about the room. Otto's young wife, her hair in braids, entered from the kitchen with a silver tray of coffee and cakes.

Otto resumed his talk. "Besides my work as huntsmaster, I am training as a soldier here," he said, dropping crumbs on the leather couch. "The Russian Empire is weakening, and we will get our independence, if only our young people stay away from socialism. Unfortunately, the same disturbances the Bolsheviks create in St. Petersburg are now going on in Helsinki."

The women couldn't fathom what he was talking about, but when Otto mentioned trouble in Helsinki, they were glad that Taisto was in America.

"Let me show you something," Otto said. He took them up the stairs along the circular balcony overlooking the big room. He pointed to the wall at the far end, above the kitchen. "Look at this." He pushed on the wall and the panel slid to the side, exposing a row of rifles mounted with bayonets.

"German," Otto said, "the best there is."

Lempi noticed how his eyes shone as he handled one of the rifles, worked the bolt back and forth, and stroked the wooden stock with the palm of his hand. How tenderly he fondles it, as if the gun were alive. How is it that men love guns? Guns, horses, women—they love their guns as much as their horses or their women. Lempi turned away and looked down over the balcony railing to the big stone fireplace.

"Let me show you something else," Otto said, and he closed the wall and took the women with the children to one of the side rooms on the balcony.

"See this?" He led them reverentially to the corner of the room, to a small table draped in white linen. On the table rested a glass-enclosed photograph framed within a spruce-bough wreath. A lighted candle flickered, reflecting off the glass. "It is my job to attend this candle," Otto said. "The man in the photograph won the honour to kill Bobrikov, and in order to avoid capture, he shot himself for the glory of Finland."

Otto's face glowed with pride and intrigue. Important people trusted him with their secrets. His superiors had planned and executed the assassination of the hated Russian Governor-General, and the secret was in his care.

Lempi squeezed Urho's little hand, then patted him on the head. She knew that soon Finland would make war against itself, that brothers would fight brothers, and she hoped that when they returned to Kuusamo there might be a letter telling Senja to go to America.

Chapter Seven

"Oho, you wretched iron you,
Miserable bog heap—and you, steel,
By some evil charm possessed!
Was it from this you were born,
Why you turned out such a terror,
Overgrew yourself so bigly?"

Kalevala, Runo 9

Senja had wanted so much to be with Taisto when Sirkku was born, but it couldn't be. Anyway, what sense was there to have a man around at a birth? Ya, what does a man know? But one thing about Taisto, he was a faithful husband—he wrote letters, thirty-one in two years, and sent money to her whenever he could. Senja painted an America of her own inside her head, all from the letters. When the ship gets to New York harbour she will watch for an Ellis Island. The famous statue is on the water close by the island, Taisto said. They will get off the ship at Ellis Island. Medical examination for clearance to the United States of America.

"Urho, look. There it is—the woman with the torch, like Father said in his letter. It is the Statue of Liberty!" She held him above the heads of the crowd, and then she held Sirkku. They had arrived. Step on the wooden ramp to this Ellis Island. Sit with the children on a bench in a big room. Everything healthy, I can go. Train tickets pinned to our clothes. Wait for the barge. Now to ask questions. Who to ask? How can I ask when I don't know this English? Where do I find this Hibbing, this Iron Range? Surely there are Finns here who know where to go.

That evening on the train it was past midnight before the children finally settled to sleep. Then she tried to sleep, but the unfamiliar train noises and her excitement kept her awake most of the night. In the morning she saw the red Mesabi. Senja read Taisto's letter for the hundredth time....

> *"Everything is red—the roads, the water*
> *in the ditches, my clothes, skin—the red*
> *ore penetrates—drives into everything. The*
> *big open pit of the mine is red—the sidewalks.*
> *Houses sit on every side of the pit—tarred-*
> *paper shacks, log huts, company barracks—*
> *all coated with the red dust, until it rains.*
> *Then everything turns to mud."*

The train stopped to take on water at Mountain Iron, four miles west of the town of Virginia, and she was able to see first hand what Taisto had said about the might of America, the greatest iron ore mine in the world. She saw a deep gouge cut into the rock earth, a hole extending so far across that the dead trees on the other side were the size of match-sticks. Far below, ore trains, five or six of them, pulled a dozen cars on different levels of terracing along the sides of the massive depression, trailing like snakes round and round down to the bottom of the excavation, back and forth like little boys' toys. One of the trains, about two hundred feet down, stopped on a terrace along the west side wall of the pit, and a steam shovel above the terrace dumped ore into its cars. There were three other steam shovels working that she could see. If Taisto thought that the Statue of Liberty represented the spirit of America, this mine at Mountain Iron, at least in Senja's eyes, represented the body, and she could never have imagined, before seeing it, how big and powerful that body was, and she was excited by her husband's part in it.

But later, when Taisto met them in the evening at the Hibbing station, she wasn't so sure. She had lived in the hope of the two of them being so happy finally to see each other again. But when she and the children got off the train, and he was standing on the crowded platform, he didn't look happy. He looked dirty and tired. He greeted Senja by holding onto her hand, and his knuckles were scabbed, his fingernails broken, and rust was deeply etched in the cracked skin of his fingers.

"I am sorry I am so filthy," Taisto said. "I got off my shift just in time to meet the train."

The children hid behind Senja's skirt. "Urho, this is your father. Sirkku, your father." Senja smiled, lowered her eyes, and squeezed his hand.

The reunited family didn't have far to walk from the train. Hibbing, like other Mesabi towns, was built on the mine site, and the workers' shacks hung almost over the edge of the open pit.

Senja, once inside the door of her new home, made a quick inventory of the meagre contents of the room—a cot, a tin stove, several wooden boxes. She looked at Taisto. He was watching her, and she began to cry, not because there was nothing in the shack, but because she read his eyes, and they told her that he thought it was not good enough for her, that he was not good enough for her.

Taisto said, "What is it now? Why are you crying?"

"I don't know—nothing is the matter, Taisto. I am just a silly woman."

"Ya, this place is not much," he said, kicking an empty packing-crate on the floor. "Water pumping engines for the mine." He then slowly read the letters stencilled on the side of the crate, faltering on each word: "Fairbanks-Morse Steam Pumps." He nodded at Senja, and his eyes didn't look quite so defeated. "I can read the English," he said. "We will use the Oliver Mining Company box for our table, if they don't kick us out of here when we strike next week."

"Strike?"

"Ya, what's the difference?" He kicked the crate again. "Look how we have to live."

Senja sat on the cot, laying the sleeping Sirkku gently down beside her. At least there was a bed. She could fix something for the children on the floor, and they'd have more bedding when her pinewood chest arrived. She should have asked Lempi to make them a rug; one of her weavings on the wall would have brought some colour to the place. She watched her son at the door. Urho was looking out at three little boys across the way, making roads in the red dirt.

Taisto sat on the cot beside his wife. He picked up the sleeping Sirkku, holding her a moment to his bristled chin, then set her down again. "Oh, I make her dirty. I don't look so good, ya, Senja?"

She grinned at him, wiping the rust on the side of his face with her hand. Both of them began laughing, slowly at first, and then more and more till they couldn't stop. They laughed and held each other, kissing each other's lips—noses, eyes, ears, necks—rusty tears covering their faces.

The strike failed. Only the Finns laid down their tools, and not all of them, only the socialists, the ones associated with the Finnish section of the Social Democratic Party, the ones who frequented the Hibbing Finn Hall. It failed too because the Oliver Mining Company was prepared for it.

At 6:30 in the morning, ten days after Senja had arrived at the Hibbing Station, Taisto was at the mine gates with a crowd of men waving banners: IWW, Western Miners' Union, and the Red Flag. At 6:50 the steam whistle blew, and the night shift began its trek out of the pit. As they went by the strikers, the men waved their lunch buckets and held their fists in the air.

Nobody was coming in for the morning shift—it appeared that the word had got around.

The strikers had barely assembled, getting ready to march from the mine gates down the front street of Hibbing to the fair grounds, when Oliver's men came. They advanced in a wide line, wielding bats and iron bars, attempting to force the strikers through the gates and corner them in the supply yard.

"Is that scabs?" Taisto asked the man beside him.

"No," the man said, grabbing a rock off the ground. "They didn't come to work, and if you don't want your head bashed in, you'd better find something to throw."

A man with a long white diagonal scar across his cheek was waving a bar above his head. That Irishman! How could this be?

"Let's get em," the Scar-face yelled, "I had my fill of these Mongolian bastards in Soudan."

Taisto backed up against a wire-mesh fence. He had nowhere to go. The Scar-face was coming at him, and all at once Taisto realized he could be killed. He had a wife and two children come all the way from Finland, and now this happens. What will happen to them if I get killed? At the Finn Hall the organizers told him to come unarmed—he didn't even have his knife, but what good was a *puukko* against a four-foot iron bar?

An hour later, two strikers brought Taisto home. Urho was playing in the ruts in front of the shack, breaking lumps of red dirt into powder. Sirkku sat beside him, sifting the powder though her tiny fingers. With a scrap of tarpaper, Urho scooped some powder into a tin can, and dumped it on Sirkku's head, making her near-white hair the colour of rust. She began to howl, but stopped when she saw her father, coming towards her, hopping on one foot, his arms around the necks of the men supporting him.

Urho remembered all his life his mother's crying, and his father's cursing. "Goddamn bosses, my kneecap's broken, Senja!" Urho was too young to understand, but somehow he knew the ugly bosses had hurt his father, and made his mother cry. He knew the bosses were no good. Little Urho grabbed his tin can, scooped it full of dirt, then set it down. He too began to cry.

Chapter Eight

Väinämöinen pondered thus:
"Who is there to plant this land,
Sow the seeds and sow them thickly"
"Pellervoinen, gnome of plowland,
Little Sampsa Pellervoinen,
He's the boy to do the planting,
Sow the seeds and sow them thickly."

Kalevala, Runo 2

After the strike business, Taisto made a decision. He would leave this Devil's land of gold, these hell-holes. Matt wrote that the farming was good in Canada—a farm for ten dollars.

The family boarded the train for Winnipeg on the 24th of June, St. John's day, 1907. To reach the Coteau in Saskatchewan, they had to change trains in Winnipeg, take the Canadian Pacific four hundred miles west to Moose Jaw, and transfer again to a line going to Saskatoon. They got off the train at Elbow, on the big bend of the Saskatchewan River.

Senja spotted Matt Inhonen among the men on the station platform. "Look, children, Matti waits for us!" and she waved at him from the window.

Such commotion there was, the railway cars unloading young people with children, young men, steamer trunks, bags of seed grain, prickly rolls of barbed wire, clean white lumber carried off the box-cars on the side track, bags of flour, boxes of apples, coffee beans, men shovelling coal out of box-cars, single-furrow ploughs in crates, bedsteads, cupboards, tables and chairs, a piano, grain wagons, a steam engine on a flat-car, screaming horses being unloaded from a box-car, cows, crates of squawking chickens, pigs.

Empty wagons, some pulled by horses, some by oxen, found a spot along the platform to load up. Loaded wagons pulled away. The train engine hissed steam at the ties and under the platform, and dumped hot sulphur-smelling cinders. Matt Inhonen bumped into people, yelling above the heads of the crowd, "Taisto, over here! Senja! My wagon!"

They loaded the wagon with Senja's pine wood chest, a roll of bedding, a box of dishes and the other few belongings the family brought from Hibbing, along with provisions Matt bought for them at the Elbow general store: a bag of oatmeal, sugar, flour, a box of coffee, a case of prunes, and some tools. A new axe and shovel were clamped to the side of the wagon-box. The morning was hot and Matt drove the wagon to the livery barn and watered the oxen. He told everybody to take a good drink at the pump, and after filling his two water jugs, off they went. Senja and the children sat on the bedding in the middle of the wagon, and Matt and Taisto rode at the front. The family saw the town quickly disappear behind them, as Matt's team lumbered down into the river hills.

The Saskatchewan River meandered far below, visible only now and again. The wagon rolled down through the brushwood as Matt reached out his right hand, holding the lever, adjusting the tension on the front wheel. In places where the drop was particularly steep, he had to get off the wagon and run a pole through the rear wheels, skidding the wagon. The oxen strained with the weight.

"It is steeper on the other side going up," Matt told Taisto, seated beside him. Taisto watched the oxen's big hooves, the knees bending, trying to resist the downward force of the wagon. "You should have seen it when we came three years ago. There were only Indian trails to follow. We get our firewood in these river brakes, and it takes a good team and driver to climb out without tipping a wagon loaded with trees."

The wagon easily crossed the foot-deep water and sandbars, and then started uphill. The oxen, more sure of themselves and eager to be out of the river hills, climbed briskly to the top without a stop.

"Now you see the Coteau," Matt announced, "Four miles we go west on this sandy flat, and then we are on those hills you see ahead of us, the Coteau Hills. In these hills are the homesteads."

The Saskatchewan homestead land was like the *Työmies* newspaper said. The paper had said the land was a rolling ocean of virgin prairie. Taisto could see it was not like the mouldy swamp reeds of his old hay meadow, but instead a mass of tangled wool, thick curls of grass. He saw no trees, only patches of scrubby brush scraping the wagon bottom. On their way across the hills he saw bones—a bleached skull, sometimes a rib, a leg bone. "That's buffalo," Matt said. They passed along the top of a steep coulee, stopping to look down at a great pile of these bones along the bottom. Matt said the settlers called this landmark 'Bone Coulee'.

Senja smelled the air. She marvelled at the fragrances, sharply cleansing, spicy. Insects hummed in the shimmering heat, bees crawled into the scanty prairie roses dotted here and there like pink patches on the buckbrush. The oxen flicked their tails, and their hides flinched, unsettling the flies.

"It is so large, this Coteau," Taisto said, "like the ocean." To the south the hills declined into a broad shimmering flat, and indeed the faraway homesteads looked like ships rolling on water as far as the eye could see.

"Those dwellings, there on the plain, do they belong to our countrymen, to Finns?"

"No," Matt said, "that is the English, some Norwegians. They got here first. But all the soil is rich, even these hills. All of it is hard like rock—you need two ox teams for the plough to break the land. But at least there are no trees to fight."

"And no stumps," said Taisto. He clenched his jaw, laughing and grinding his teeth at the same time. "Minnesota is like Finland— nothing but stump farms."

He couldn't beat that fish pedlar's stupid farm at Lempi's but Taisto was sure he could beat this Coteau. The work was tough, but he could win. By the end of October he had ploughed more than the ten acres the Homestead Act required— "proving up," the government called it. He was the owner of one hundred and sixty acres of land, not the fish pedlar's seven acres of swamp. Never had he seen soil like this Coteau. Dig a well and there was good soil to the bottom, hard like rock, but rich, all the way down. Tenho Maki said some farms in Minnesota, where it rained all the time, had soft soil like a fish's belly. The Mesabi mining land was no fish belly, Taisto thought. The Mesabi was like Finland, rocks like fish heads. Lots of rain in Finland, but the soil was no good. Nothing could match this Coteau.

Taisto used Tenho's plough and ox team, matching them up with two oxen borrowed from Matt Inhonen. He got up at sunrise day after day and ploughed the land. His knee ached from sitting on that bouncing plough seat. His neck ached from looking down to watch the blade cut the sod. But it was something, the way the sod lifted, all the time resisting the forward and upward pull of the blade. The sod moved like a ripple on water, like the flanks of oxen, flesh moving across the bone. He could see the coulter disc roll into the sod, cutting just ahead of the ploughshare, like a knife slicing a boil. In Minnesota he had seen a plough cut with a rigid knife instead of a rolling disc. But such a thing could not stand up to this Coteau turf.

Sometimes the oxen bolted because of the heel flies. One day the lead ox, a big one-horned black with a white patch on his left eye, veered to the right and kept walking straight into a slough. Of course the others followed. Taisto was dumbfounded, too surprised to jump off. The plough dragged across the furrows. He tugged at the lines and swore at the beasts, but nothing would stop them, and mounted on the bouncing plough he was pulled into the slough. He felt foolish perched like a cuckoo bird with his boots bobbing in the water, while ahead of him a duck quacked and took flight.

How could this happen to him? He was thankful only that no one was there to see him in his predicament. All four oxen were lying in the water, and Taisto helplessly pulled on the lines while pondering what he should do. The patch-eyed ox paid him no mind, and his big tongue pulled at a bulrush.

Taisto leaped off the plough seat into the water and sloshed his way to the front of the team. "The Patch-eye led these bastards in and he can lead them out," he said, loud enough for anyone to hear, but only the oxen were present. He grabbed the ox's halter and tugged. He would not budge. Taisto tugged on one ox after another, several times, and none would even lift its head, or stop eating the bulrushes. He grabbed the lines and then whipped the Patch-eye across his shoulders and on the nose—still nothing. Matt had told him how stubborn these animals were, and for sure not to let them get into a slough. Sure, don't let them go to the slough—but how do you stop them? Matt told him that one day when the oxen stopped pulling and just stood in the one spot eating prairie grass, he got so angry that he hit the Patch-eye on the head with a hammer to get it moving.

Taisto had no hammer. Ah, but he had his *puukko* in his boot. He would fix this son of a bitch. Ya, what do you think, Patch-eye, do you want your ears? He poked the animal's bony forehead with the tip of his knife, and it shook its head and tugged at another bulrush. So you think you can win, ya, we will see. I need some beef this coming winter, ya? Then what would you think? Hah? One-horn?

Taisto stared at the ox, eye to eye. He grabbed its ear and cut a one-inch rip. The animal was instantly up on his feet, jerking at the harness, and pulling the others, with Taisto alongside holding the lines, and splashed out of the slough with the plough.

Taisto worked as if possessed. He worked on that prairie till freeze-up. And he worked alone. Saskatchewan was such a big open space, summer and winter. His homestead was fourteen miles southwest from the river. Matt Inhonen's claim was in a deep valley, three miles further southwest, and Tenho Maki was three miles southeast, closer to the river. A bachelor by the name of Pikku Juntinen was Taisto's nearest neighbour, his sod shack visible on a hill half a mile south of Taisto's homestead. Being alone out here he could feel so powerful, and yet so helpless and puny against the sky. Sometimes he could stretch up and reach for the sky. Other times, like other living things, he welcomed the protection of shelter. The plants and animals behaved against the wind and sky in ways he had not seen in Finland. Evergreen shrubs lay flat on the ground. He had never seen a tree grow in such a way, if he could call it a tree. It had branches like the juniper in Finland, but it lay in mats on the hillside. The prairie wool, as Matt called the virgin grass, hugged the ground, curled over, making shelters for mice to rear their little ones and to hide from hawks. Their nests in the prairie wool kept them warm throughout the cold winter. Even Taisto's sod shack hugged the ground.

Taisto welcomed the winter. From Tenho Maki he got potatoes, and he and Matt brought wagon-loads of firewood from the river hills. He brought good maple hardwood to carve. He made chairs and a loom for Senja, completing the loom before December. Senja tore rags into strips and used them to weave three rugs for the floor, and another to hang on the wall. She had seen an ad in *Työmies* for expensive dyes and wool to make fancy rugs. Maybe when they could afford it she would send for some. Beside her home-made rugs she hung a Massey-Harris calendar from the blacksmith in town. On the calendar was a picture of a rosy-cheeked young woman wearing a sun-bonnet. On the other wall was another calendar; this one was from Pringle's General Store, a picture of a girl in a cowboy hat and red neck scarf. These girls in the calendars looked so cheerful and bright—so much colour with sunlight streaming through apple tree boughs, and big red apples hanging, green grass and flowers. Each day Senja marked off the dates on both calendars.

"Pikku Juntinen is having people over tonight to bring in the new year," Senja said. "Imagine, 1908. Shouldn't we go? I am sick of making rugs."

"I don't know," Taisto said, "it will be mostly politics. Haven't you heard Matt speak before? I'd like to stay at home and finish this chair." He sat by the stove, a maple rung in one hand and a rasp in the other.

Four-year-old Urho was on the bed with Sirkku, playing with a jar of buttons. He heard his mother, and he watched to see what his father would do. Urho wanted to go. He wanted to play with Matt Inhonen's boy, Paul.

Taisto slowly worked the rasp. "Pikku is having the meeting at his place because he wants to form an organization, and before you know it we'll be asked for money for memberships and to build a hall."

He remembered that day at the mine, the man with the scar. What did the Finns and the organizations do for him? What did they get him? A smashed knee. To hell with them and their meetings, and to hell with the mines. What could be more satisfying then staying at home carving the wood, not having to hear the steam whistle shrieking at 6:30 in the morning rousing the miners to work? The only steam whistle he heard on the Coteau was from Matt's engine on his threshing outfit, which he blew to scare Pikku Juntinen who was pitching sheaves from the rack.

"Come on, Taisto," Senja pleaded, "this is not Hibbing, and Matt is not going on strike. We haven't heard singing for a long time, and the children need others to play with. Matt will bring his son Paul."

"Ya, and Ruth will stay home. She is the only one with any sense."

But Taisto knew he wasn't being fair to Senja, and was thinking only about himself—about how good it was to farm here, not like that stupid swamp in Finland. He had not thought about how Senja might feel being cooped up all winter, and that she might be missing Lempi. He should be taking her places, maybe on the sleigh to Tenho Makis' to get the mail.

"Ya, why not, Senja. We need the fresh air, so maybe get the children dressed."

"I have baked some prune tarts this afternoon. I will take them, Taisto."

Senja and Taisto skied the half mile to Pikku's place, pulling the children behind them on sleds. In Finland, skiing had been easier. Here the snow was dry and hard, wind-blown, polished by ground-drift snaking in waves on the hard-packed surface. Taisto struggled with his stiff knee and his right ski kept slipping on the ice. Senja glided ahead of him, her skirts flapping, skiing with reckless ease. She stopped, looked back, and waited.

They could hear coyotes yapping, a chorus of yelps and howls. Urho covered his face with his mitts and peeked out with one eye. To the west a faint light outlined the top of the hills. The east was completely black, and it felt to him as if the unseen mass of hills were lunging forward, rolling toward him like a bumpy muscle along the hidden bottom of the sky.

Senja and Taisto struggled up the hill, pulling the sleds to Pikku's shack. They saw the closed-in cutters and the open grain wagons with blanketed horses tethered to them. Off to one side, somebody's ox, tied to a stoneboat, munched on an oat sheaf. Taisto and Senja unfastened their skis and set them alongside several others propped against the soddie.

Inside, the room was scented with coal-oil, tobacco, boiling coffee, wood fire, and earth. The meeting had started. Seated on planks, the group of twenty or thirty people faced Matt Inhonen.

"We need someone to record the proceedings," Matt said.

"I choose Hilja Mukari," Pikku Juntinen said. He pursed his lips, then puffed on his cigarette.

"And what about a chairman?" Hilja said.

"Ya, Matti, you do just fine," Pikku said, and puffed again. He rose to his feet. "I think we should talk about building a hall," he said, "and first we must raise the money for the lumber."

"Why not sod?" Taisto said. "We build our houses out of sod."

"A hall is too big to make with the sods, Taisto, even

if we plough them from the slough edge. It doesn't matter how tough the sod hangs together. If it's stacked too high the wall will lean."

Hilja Mukari laid her pen down on her open ledger book. She was a thick-necked woman. Having worked in a brickyard in Finland, she was muscled across the shoulders and arms. "All this jabber about a hall. This kind of thundering is nothing but *Hall Socialism!*" Hilja grabbed her pen and pointed at Pikku. "We bake the pies and do all this quilting? Sell the tickets? All this to build a hall for the dances and outsiders to get drunk? That is what the *Hall Socialism* is. It will not bring about the final victory. Read your *Työmies*."

"Ya," a few in the crowd called out, and Hilja continued. "The women have better causes for the money than to build a hall!"

"I don't know," Pikku said, "As long as the woman sleeps in the same bed as the man, the two should work together. Without a hall we cannot organize. Look how crowded we are already in my shack. For sure we need the hall. Where should we build it?"

Senja listened excitedly to all the talk about a hall, and then she thought of something Lempi had said back in Finland, something Senja had not understood. When a letter had come from Taisto describing how the Finns in America built all these halls, Lempi had said that even in Finland some people think they must have dance halls. But the young are even more lost when they are far away across the ocean, far away in a land of strange tongues. Lempi had said just wait and see. They build these halls, make plays, read books, and think they will get to know everything. They will know, all right, soon enough what God will do when they build a Tower of Babel.

Chapter Nine

I am wanting, I am thinking
To arise and go forth singing,
Sing my songs and say my sayings,
Hymns ancestral harmonizing,
Lore of kindred Lyricking.

Kalevala, Runo 1

Leave Finland? Lempi thought about it much of the time. Why would anybody want to leave Finland to go to a dry prairie? For those young people it was different, but her? Why should she go?

Why not? Why not go to Taisto? Eight long years she missed him, and she wanted to see her brother Tenho yet in this life. Senja's letters tell how Taisto is helping to build a hall. Why can't Taisto help his Uncle Tenho build a church instead? No, the young people these days would rather build dance halls, even in Finland. Ya, she will go to Canada, get to see Senja and the children again. So long ago they left. Would she even recognize them?

It was haying time when Tenho Maki's big team of Percherons entered the yard. On the wagon were his wife, Maria, the children, Fred and Eva, and Tenho at the front beside his sister Lempi.

Lempi sat a moment before getting down from the wagon, enjoying the smell of the newly-cured hay stacked by the henhouse, and admiring Taisto's and Senja's new wood-frame house with its shingled walls and roof, and a porch with a small window shaped like a diamond on the door.

A red clucker hen crossed in front of the horses with

nine chicks in tow. Fred raced after them, Urho followed, and Sirkku pulled Eva along by the hand.

"They're under the sulky plough!" Fred yelled, "By the henhouse." The children ran to Fred and grouped around close. Transformed to twice her size, her feathers fussing out like jets of fire, her body levitating, thrusting forward, her beak clicking, the hen turned on them. The boys and Sirkku ran, but Eva was trapped against the henhouse wall.

Lempi squinted against the sun, her eyes pinched upward at the corners. For a big woman, she stepped lightly. She climbed down from the wagon, sure of foot, walked to the hen, bent over it and touched her fingers to its ruffled collar. Slowly the feathers settled and Lempi stroked along the wings. The bird relaxed, shrank. She picked it up, set it among the chicks under the plough, and taking Eva's hand, walked smiling to the house.

Senja seated Lempi in a rocking chair in the middle of the kitchen. Tenho and Maria sat at the table by the window, and the four children stood beside the kitchen doorway. Senja couldn't stand still. She rubbed her hands together, held them to her blushing face, pulled at her apron, and clapped. "Oh, Lempi! You have come to Canada. What do you think?"

"It is a long ride on the train. Where is Taisto?"

Senja stepped back. Hadn't Tenho said anything? He should know that Lempi would understand. "Taisto is helping the men set rafters on the new hall this morning. He didn't want to go, but before he knew which day you were arriving he had promised Matt. He should be home at any time. Now tell us about your trip."

"The train, oh yes. When the ship came to that place, what is it? Halifax? I thought I had arrived here, but no. The train journey covers so much country. What can I tell you about this Canada when there is too much to say?"

"What about here?" Senja said. "What do you think about our farm?"

"You have a big house."

"Ya, Lempi. We have a special room for you. The

children sleep upstairs. Tell us what you see here that is different from Finland."

Lempi didn't hesitate. "The sky," she said.

She rocked back and forth in the chair, the toes of her black boots showing below her mottled green print dress. A black knitted shawl draped her shoulders, and she wore a coarse linen head-scarf. On the floor beside her was a bag made from the same linen. "Yes, it is the sky that is different." Her shadowy eyes moved around the kitchen, then slowly she rose, eyeing the children. She turned and walked towards the rug hanging on the wall beside the curtained doorway by the stove. "The colours, Senja. You have the sun in this rug." She walked through the doorway into a sun-filled room. On the windows flies buzzed, the big ones thumping on the panes, and more of them circled zapping on the screen-door. She stepped outside and raised her head to the sky. "The yellow sun has so much room." Never had she seen the sun so bright against the sky. And the sky was round, like inside a duck egg. But there was something about this sky that was the same as Finland. It reminded her of the times she walked in the snow mists to cut the hole for washing clothes. She could not explain how this blue sky could feel to her like the snow mist and dark ice of her lake.

This sky was not gloomy like the Finland winter, and how could something as brilliant as this wide open sight above remind her of gloom? The big sky and the big lake. Maybe that's it—the lonely sky and the lonely lake. When she dipped her wash up and down in the hole, and pounded the clothing on the ice and dipped again, then wrung out the icy water, she knew she was alone.

The clucker hen scratched in the loose dirt along the side of the house, burrowed into it, bathed in the dust, and the nine chicks scurried in and out from under its wings. Lempi walked around the corner, entering the house through the back porch, and into the kitchen to her rocking chair. So nice to rock. Taisto is good with the knife to make the chairs, good with the wood, like the men in Finland. Ya, this is a big country, and the young people alone out here, and the children. But not one tree is there for someone to hide from the sun.

"What are you thinking?" Tenho asked. His hand shook as he poured coffee from his cup into his saucer and sipped. "Are you lost somewhere in your thoughts?"

"Oh, no, no, Tenho. I think of the children. The little girl, Eva, your step-child. Such nice dark hair."

"Ya," Tenho said.

"A shy girl." She eyed the children again. "How old are you, Eva?"

The mother, Maria, wrung her hands, gazing up for a moment. "Eight years, coming nine," she said. Little Eva's eyes closed, her head hung. Fred nudged his elbow into her side, and Sirkku giggled.

With his eyes on Lempi's bag Fred moved away from the wall. He reached out his foot, kicked the cloth, toppling something inside that clunked. The boy drew away as Tenho raised his hand and gestured for him to quit snooping and go outside. Fred ran into the porch, and Urho set the bag straight and followed. The girls waited a moment, then went out too.

Lempi asked Senja, "Shouldn't Taisto be raking the hay?"

"Oh, he works so hard at the farming. It is good for him to have something else."

"Ah," Tenho said, "Taisto hears the politics all the time, Pikku Juntinen jabbering, and Matt. They should be carpenters, not farmers. All this month they are building, all the socialists. They build this hall for their meetings, and for dancing."

"Oh, but they will have plays, too," Senja said. "The plays will be something to see, Lempi."

"Political plays," Tenho said, "Many Finns come here from the Mesabi country, angry miners from the strikes."

"Taisto wrote to me about the mines. How is his knee?"

Senja laughed. "When it aches he is grouchy, and he walks like his joints need oiling. But he walked like that before. My goodness, Lempi, you must be starved from the trip. We should eat."

"An old woman doesn't have to eat, but maybe the children are hungry."

"Pancakes and salt fish before sauna—tomorrow we have chicken. Taisto will butcher a rooster."

At that moment the porch door opened and shut. Taisto swatted dust from his pantlegs and stepped into the kitchen. Nobody spoke. Everyone looked at Lempi and then back at Taisto.

"Hello, Mother," Taisto said.

Lempi began to rise, but Taisto motioned for her to remain seated. He approached, reached for her hand. Lempi sat forward, her eyes glistening. Taisto held her hand, and looked into her eyes. "Ya, Mother, you don't get younger after eight years."

"Bah," she said. "Why don't you look at yourself?" Her head shook a little, and the wrinkles at the corners of her mouth extended upward as she smiled. "I am only forty-six."

"Is there coffee?" Taisto said, turning to Senja and pulling a chair up to the table. Senja placed a cup with a saucer in front of him. Taisto reached for the lump sugar, and carefully spilled coffee into his saucer.

"How is the hay coming?" Tenho asked and cleared his throat.

"Ya, it waits," Taisto said, "We shingle the hall roof tomorrow." From his pocket he took a flat oval can of Prince Albert tobacco and filled his pipe. He struck a match on his thumbnail.

Senja fingered her apron. "Maria," she said, "come to the garden. I'd like you to look at the potatoes—some kind of bug. Maybe you or Tenho might know what to do. Oh, yes, and, Taisto, when you get time kill the biggest rooster for tomorrow's dinner. Get the boys to catch it."

The two sat alone. Taisto held his pipe up, clicked the stem on his teeth.

"Ya, Mother. It is a long time."

"You have a nice farm. Nice house. Nice family."

Taisto walked to the stove and poured himself coffee. "When you left home, Mother, were they cutting hay in the meadow?"

"Ya, just starting, but it is raining all spring there," she said, rocking slowly back and forth, "And the hay rots, even on the raised stacks."

Lempi pointed to the window. "My goodness—one can see far in this country. Whose is that place to the south?"

"Pikku? Ya, you will have to meet him. Pikku Juntinen, he is a bachelor."

"Bah!" Lempi said. "You think I want to meet a bachelor at my age?"

"Say, Mother. Do you think this afternoon you could give me a treatment? My knee bothers me, and maybe a massage will do it some good."

"I bring my things from Finland," she said. "Maybe your knee needs more than just a massage. Maybe the blood gets bad in America, and you need *kuppaus.*" She patted her linen-cloth bag. "Maybe a good blood-letting will make your knee feel better."

"Ya, I am happy that you come to Canada. Let's go get that rooster."

Fred met them in the porch, shielding his face with one hand, and holding the legs of the rooster with the other.

"Well, well, look at this." Taisto took the flapping bird from the boy. "I can get to work now," he said, and carried the rooster across the yard to the chopping block. Fred followed closely, and Urho and the girls went to watch from behind the woodpile.

The rooster squawked and flapped, with its head jutting out stiffly. With his free hand Taisto lifted the axe above the block. *Thump!* The partially severed head lay on the stump, and again Taisto struck with the axe. The rooster shot forward as Taisto let go of its feet, blood spurting from the wiggling neck. The remnant of neck on the detached head jerked twice and the head fell to the ground. Bloody feathers stuck to the blade of the axe. The headless rooster ran at Urho, and the boy scampered up the woodpile. The bird banged against the stacked wood and turned, running here and there. Fred ran with it, back and forth, against the sauna door, and back to the chopping block. Then at last the bird flopped over, legs kicking out, claws scraping the hard dirt, wings beating the dust, the throbbing neck slapping at the ground. Finally the thrashing of the neck slowed to spastic jerks, and stopped.

"Take this to the house," Taisto said, picking it up, and extended his hand to Urho who was standing on the woodpile. Urho stared at the severed head, spattered with blood and dirt, lying beside the chopping block.

Fred held out his hand.

"Ya," Taisto said, "you take it," and he laughed, jutting his chin out to the side, and wiping the axe in the grass.

By late afternoon Taisto had heated the sauna and prepared himself for his mother's treatment. Protecting his eyes from the biting smoke, he climbed to the high bench and threw several dippers of water onto the cairn-like pile of rocks on the floor. The fire had burned out, but for several hours a roaring woodfire had heated the rocks, and now the steam drove out the smoke. Soon his body gleamed with sweat. The heat grabbed at his ribs, enticing out the dirt, the sawdust, the itch from the hay-fields, even the memories of rusty dirt. He steamed for twenty minutes, then climbed off the bench and lay with his head on his arms, on a low platform near the sauna door.

Fred and Urho were watching ants crawling on the rooster head, and then they spotted Lempi entering the sauna.

"Is there a window to peek through?" Fred asked.

"Ya," Urho said, "At the side. But they might see us."

"Nah, we'll be quiet," Fred said, leading the way.

The sauna was dug into an earth bank, and the boys circled from around the woodpile, approaching from the top of the hill to the window at the side. Through the clouded glass they saw Lempi shake a *vasta* over the hot stones, then slap it many times across Taisto's back and legs. Then she put the wet branches into a bucket of water on the low bench, and began massaging his back, and his bad leg, hammering, then kneading with her strong hands.

Ya, Lempi thought, smiling to herself—those boys are watching. They don't know what is the *kuppaus?* Young boys in a young country, different country than Finland. Will there be no more *kuppaus?* Maybe it is good that they see. She stopped her massage and, opening her bag, reached inside and drew out a small mallet, putting it on the bench beside her. Then she reached back into the bag, took out six cow horns, carefully, one at a time—each horn with a hole on its tip. With a knife she cut a turnip into six cubes.

With the mallet she tapped at Taisto's back, and the bad leg. It was her father's mallet—maybe a hundred years old, a mallet of needles. She tapped with the needles and soon droplets of blood appeared like sweat along Taisto's back.

"Look at the blood!" Fred whispered to Urho, whose eyes widened.

She next cupped one of the horns on Taisto's back, leaned over, placed her lips on the horn's tip and sucked, then quickly skewered a cube of turnip on the tip of the horn. She did the same with the others, placing them along his back, and then she put one on Taisto's bad knee.

"Hey, she's coming out!" Fred said, and they ran uphill. Lempi stood outside the door, took off her white babushka and wiped her sweaty face and forearms. She left Taisto in the sauna for half an hour, then went back inside and removed a horn from below his shoulder-blade. The cow horn was filled with blood, and it spilled along his back. Each one in turn was filled with blood.

"Let's get out of here," Fred whispered, and they ran up the hill.

From the sauna window Lempi watched them run. Ya, it will be hard for these boys, the old and the new, what to take, what to leave. It will be bad for them—they won't keep the old, they will laugh at the old ways, and the people of this new country will laugh at them.

Ya, it was bad for them at school, and Pikku Juntinen didn't make it better. What won't a man do sometimes! How stupid! The day before the new school opened, Urho and Fred went to snare gophers in Pikku's pasture. They took him a loaf of fresh *pulla,* baked in the morning. Taisto always said that nobody made coffee bread as good as his mother's.

"So, it's off to the school tomorrow," Pikku said. He led the boys to his tool-shed to get twine for their snares. "What do you know about speaking the English?"

"Nothing," Fred answered, speaking for both boys.

"You will have to learn," Pikku said. "I know many words. Let's get the twine then we'll go to the house. I'll teach you what to say to the teacher. It is best to make a good first impression at school."

The next morning a couple dozen children, the girls in dresses and hair braided in pig-tails and ribbon, the boys with their hands in pockets and caps on their tanned and scrubbed heads, stood about in clusters in front of the school. A group of English boys laughed and pointed at the Finns. Fred kicked dirt and spit at them. A tall boy chucked a rock, missing Urho's head. Then the teacher came out onto the steps of the school.

She was young. Her hair was combed back tight in a bun, and her black dress buttoned up to the neck. From the step she scanned the yard, then rang the bell in swooping motions with her hand.

"Line up," she said. "Boys in one line, girls in another."

The English boys and girls took command of the Finns, arranging the queues. As the children waited, the teacher walked up and down. She came to Fred. "And what is your name, young man?"

Fred's mouth gaped and he lowered his head, looking to the dirt at his feet.

"Young man," she repeated in a kind voice, "what is your name?"

Fred kept his eyes to the ground, removed his cap and bowed slightly. "Kiss my ass," he said. He looked up, scared.

The teacher frowned, then smiled. "I don't understand," she said. "You must speak slowly and clearly. How about your friend?" she turned to Urho. "What is your name?"

Urho looked to the ground, shuffled his boots in the dirt, dug his hands deep in his pockets. "Kiss my ass," he said.

The rock-throwing English boy laughed out loud. Others snickered. The teacher stepped back, glared at everybody, one at a time, and the laughing stopped.

"Into the school," she said. "Find any seat. I'll seat you properly when I get your names."

Voi, voi, those poor young boys, Lempi thought. The night before Urho had scrubbed extra hard to be clean for the teacher. He had gone to bed after sauna, reciting to himself the words he had memorized, and woke in the morning going over Pikku's English—'kiss my ass. kiss my ass.' Later, when Taisto heard about it, and told Urho the meaning of 'kiss my ass', the boy couldn't understand why Pikku Juntinen would do this. Senja told Taisto he should do something about that Pikku. Taisto laughed.

The English boys at school laughed at Fred and Urho. Nearly every recess the rock-throwing bully would ask them, "What's your name, boys? What's your name?" Then he would laugh. One day Urho and Fred raised their fists. "Kiss my ass!" they shouted, and then there was a fight. Always there were fights at school, English and Finns. This they learned at school. They hoped to quit school as soon as their parents would let them. Pikku said it was just as well they did quit. He said Hilja Mukari told him that schools in Canada served the interests of the ruling classes. Ya, Lempi thought, just what they need— more help from Pikku Juntinen. The life in this new country wasm't easy for these boys.

Chapter Ten

Pregnant in the treeless country,
On the open twigless barrens,
Ground ungreened by turf or tussock.
Bore her womb, her painful belly,
Carried it for two, three, four months;
For the full nine months she bore it.

Kalevala, Runo 45

Death sits in a dark hole somewhere resting, and just when it is forgotten, out it comes, even in this new country. Did I come to Canada to bury my son and his wife? Why are the young people taken? The wagon tips at the river, in the hills. And what about the children, little Sirkku, and Urho? Should they know about death? They will have to know, but how can anyone help eleven- and twelve-year-olds face the death?

Tenho had sold a team of horses to Taisto, Percherons, a fast pair of two-year-old colts. Taisto was stubborn, and he ignored Tenho's advice to get used to the team before taking it any place. He drove the horses down into the river hills for a load of wood. Senja went with him.

It was Matt Inhonen who found them at the bottom of a two-hundred foot drop, half-way down to the river. The horses were still alive, tipped on their sides, struggling in their harness, one with a broken front leg, the other with the splintered wagon tongue pierced through its belly like a skewer. He had to shoot them.

Lempi was drawing water from the well when Matt walked up the hill into the yard.

"A terrible thing has happened," Matt said.

Lempi sensed that someone had died. Ya, she was

needed to dress the dead, a bad job in summer. She wondered who it was. She could wash the body in the empty granary west of the barn. Better to work outside in the fresh air. Taisto has *Formaline,* part of a gallon in the porch left over from treating the wheat. *Formaline* will be good to wash away the smell, and it brings the colour back to the skin.

Matt said nothing. He stammered, blinking over and over. Lempi could see this was not an ordinary death. "Don't you have horses? Why do you walk here, Matti?"

"An accident, Taisto and Senja...."

"Where are they?"

"I left the wagon by the barn, Lempi."

She tore off running. No, it mustn't be. My son is dead? And Senja? Lempi saw the boxes on the wagon. Then she saw the children walking on the road from school. *Voi voi,* what is there to do? What can I tell them?

When Urho saw Lempi he sensed that something was terribly wrong and he felt a choking lump in his throat. He remembered just then, before anyone talked or moved, that moment in front of their shack at Hibbing when he was sitting on the road pouring red dirt on Sirkku's head—and then his father's leg dangling before his eyes, father groaning, kneecap, broken kneecap, his mother crying. Urho had not forgotten that fear, and it came back when he looked into Lempi's eyes, and at Matt Inhonen and the sag in his jaw. Urho saw the two long wooden boxes in the back of Matt's wagon.

"Your mother and father," Lempi said, "They... they...." She wrung her hands, took half a step.

Urho put his arm around Sirkku. Lempi saw the boy clench his teeth, saw his eyes squinting, blinking. Then he broke into tears.

"Mother and Father," he said.

No one ever knew what really happened, only that Taisto and Senja were dead. Lempi put together bits and pieces of the story, mostly from what she heard from Pikku Juntinen when he came to help with chores. Tenho often came.

Pikku said that Taisto shouldn't have taken the colts to the river. A wagon bouncing down into those coulees could have flushed a pheasant, and that would make any horse bolt, but with two-year-olds, even a rabbit might spook them. Taisto was heavy with the whip too, Pikku said.

He talked about everything except the deceased couple and was more interested in the technical aspects of horses and wagons, or maybe it was simply easier to talk about horses.

Tenho decided that the accident was caused from harness problems. "It takes a long time for a young horse to get used to all those straps. Taisto probably had the breeching set too low. It should be set high on the rump so that going downhill the horse's hips carry the weight of the wagon. Not the back legs." Pikku agreed. He had once seen a Norwegian from Elbow take his team down a hill that wasn't even that steep. The breeching was so low on those horses that they were set on their rear-ends halfway down the hill. He told how his own team, being harness-broke, were so used to the breeching straps that they would lean back and sit in them, taking a rest. That trick made money for Pikku at the grain elevator. When the wagon was on the scales, his team would lean back, sitting against the breeching, and he'd get an extra fifteen bushels when the agent weighed the load.

But then Tenho changed his mind. Breeching straps braked a wagon going downhill, and served no purpose whatsoever on the way up. Tenho was certain that Viktor's wagon toppled while coming up the hill, not down, since the horses were pulling a loaded wagon. He still couldn't imagine, though, the Percherons losing their footing, unless they had spotted a rattlesnake on the trail; that could have happened.

Lempi thought that never again in her lifetime could she feel so terrible a death burden as that moment beside the wagon, but a little more than two years later, Christmas time, 1918, the burden came again. This time it was the Matt Inhonen family.

When the Influenza came, Ruth was the first Finnish woman from the area who volunteered to work in the hospital set up in the Dunblane School. Lempi didn't go. She wanted to but she was shy because she couldn't speak English.

"Don't go, Ruth," she said, "you are pregnant. There are many to help at the hospital. Those English women have nothing else to do."

Ruth wouldn't listen.

Matt was upset but he didn't say anything. He worried about her. It had been fourteen years since Paul was born, and that was too long between babies. On top of this, he was going out East to Hancock, Toronto, to the Mesabi towns to speak, and also he was a delegate to the Port Arthur Convention. He'd be gone three weeks. Paul was old enough to feed the cattle and horses, and milk the cows, but what if the baby came early?

He hadn't told Ruth about his trip. He felt guilty about going. When she told him about the hospital work, he saw this as an opportunity to tell her he was going. He knew he should stay, but something drove him. He couldn't explain this even to himself—he would go and that was all there was to it. Ruth would be nursing at Dunblane most of the time anyway.

She could not tell him in words how she felt about his going, but a cold and detached glint in her eye was enough to remind him and keep his guilt alive.

One week before Christmas, five days before Matt was to be back, the weather turned. A storm hit, and when it cleared, the temperature dropped.

In the morning Urho watered the horses, a grey gelding and a roan mare. Then he hitched them to the sleigh. He was taking Lempi into town for groceries.

Lempi, in felt boots and buffalo coat, came from the house, her feet careful on the icy snow, her body wobbling sideways, her breath fogging the curls of the heavy collar. "Urho," she called.

He pulled on a strap, securing a blanket on the big grey. It was eight miles to Dunblane and the wind was cold.

Lempi walked up close to him. "Urho, I have had a dream," she said. He turned to her, and a shiver ran through his

his dreams long ago. During the time when we ate the famine bread, he said that in his dream the death spirit came and told him who would die."

Urho tugged again on the strap.

"The signs in my dream are as my father told me. I saw an oven with a pan of red meat inside. A woman, with her boy watching, reached for the pan of meat, dripping blood on the floor."

One of the mare's ears was caught under the bridle and Urho pulled it free. He patted the animal's long nose, rubbing it with his mittened hand.

"Ruth is the woman in my dream, Urho."

He continued stroking the horse's head, and taking his mitt off, combed the roan's white mane with his fingers. As far as he knew, Ruth and Paul were well. He hadn't been over to see them since Matt left for the East, but surely Tenho Maki had been there. But maybe not. It was six miles across country from Tenho's to Matt Inhonen's farm.

"Ya," Urho said, walking over to climb into the sleigh box. "It is a good thing I have hitched the team. Give me your hand, Grandma—I will help you up. We go there."

It was bitterly cold. Lempi sat on a pile of straw, with her back against the front of the box, holding the collar of her big coat over her face.

Urho stood in the sleigh, watching the horses. He held the lines in his mitt, his tweed cap pulled over his ears, his head only slightly turned from the wind. Lempi listened to the constant chinging of the harness chains, and the crunch of the iron runners on the wind-packed snow.

Ground-drift whipped through the horse's legs and swept up at their heads. Through sky-filled eddies of snow as fine as grain dust, the sun filtered its cold rays, cutting the swirling haze with sharp pillars of light.

Urho saw Tenho Maki from the top of the valley. Lempi stood up in the sleigh box and she too saw him far below, standing outside the door of Matt's house, bare-headed, his coat open and tearing at the wind. They could see him walking a few steps to his sledge, to his favourite solid-black Percheron clearly visible in the whiteness. He stood by the horse a minute, then moved back to the door of the house. There he hesitated, then turned around facing the sledge.

Urho's team pulled up beside the giant black. They climbed down from the sleigh, Lempi moving quickly to her brother. Urho stood back, his eyes darting from Tenho, to the house, to the sledge.

Tenho gazed at Lempi. "Ruth. It is my Ruth." His head, and his mouth trembled. "I can't go back in," he said.

Lempi put her mittened hands on Tenho's shoulders. Tenho's head shook. He pointed over to his sledge. On it was a frozen corpse, arms and legs and head bent askew. Barefooted, clad only in underwear, a boy lay on the floor of the sledge, stiffly sprawled like a stump ripped from the earth.

"Paul," Tenho said. "The fever must have made him crazy. I found him in the snow a mile from the house."

Both Lempi and Tenho turned their gaze quickly away, he towards the dwelling—she, to Urho.

"Ruth is inside," Tenho said. "Please. Can you do something? Can you go in?"

"Ya." Lempi said. She held him by the shoulders a moment longer, then gently rocked him back and forth, looking at the terror in his eyes. She then nodded at Urho and he followed her through the door.

Ruth was in the bedroom. Something had broken the window and the curtain snapped in the wind as skiffs of dry snow blew in across the bed. On the floor was a bucket with frozen vomit and blood streaked down its sides. Beside the pail the Eaton's catalogue lay open with a torn page flapping back and forth.

She was still alive.

She lay without blankets, her flannel nightdress drawn away from her distended body. She sensed someone in the room, and her hands clutched at her gown. She attempted to cover herself. Ruth's fingernails were blue, and her puffed lips the same ugly bloated blue. Even her eyes, mad with fever, were the same dead blue.

She was terribly bloated, and her body shook, weak in its helpless labour. The bedsheet was wet and bloody. Lempi didn't know what to do. Ruth's knees jerked upward, thighs trembled, the back arched, her body rolled from side to side. Blood drained from between her legs. Her face had turned white, and her entire body trembled, the skin wet. Moans gurgled from her throat. She gagged, choked, and then a jolting shiver hit her body, and she was dead.

Chapter Eleven

First he cleared the crown away,
Then he cut the trunk in sections,
Out of which he shaped the keelbeams
And a stack of countless lumber
For the mighty singer's vessel,
For the boat of Väinämöinen.

Kalevala, Runo 16

Pikku Juntinen waited at the station for Matt's train to come in. The pot-bellied stove was beginning to warm the cramped waiting room. Other farmers sat beside Pikku on the wooden bench, waiting for their cream cans to arrive from the Moose Jaw Creamery. Normally Pikku would have been leading them in conversation, but this morning he didn't feel like talking.

Pikku often met the train. How many minutes late? Who was getting off and on? What's the number on the engine? The big steamer coming in was like a celebration every morning. But not this time.

Pikku went out to the platform. The whistle chilled the still morning air, once, twice, three times, and then the engine appeared, big and strong, puffing steam, the arms on its iron wheels lunging forward, the railbed heaving.

Matt Inhonen, wearing a tweed cap and heavy dark overcoat, holding a black suitcase, descended from the passenger car. Pikku walked up to meet him, and then a strange thing happened.

Matt refused Pikku's offer of a ride home, and instead, without saying a word, he left Pikku standing on the platform, and set off walking the thirteen miles to his farm.

For the next few weeks the Finnish community was in

a stir. Hearing what Matt Inhonen had done at the Dunblane station, nobody knew whether to visit him or not. No one saw him anywhere, not even at the hall. Later, the one time he did appear in Dunblane that winter, he wouldn't talk to anybody— just went to the post office, then to Pringle's General Store where he loaded up on a few supplies, and skied home.

In the spring Pikku was able to visit him, but Matt wouldn't talk about how he was feeling. All he would say was something about a plan he had in mind. Pikku went to see him once or twice after that.

Matt's plan became known the following summer. One Saturday morning while Pikku was at the station watching the drayman unload lumber, Matt drove up with his team.

"Ya, Matti," Pikku said. "You build something?" The tone of Pikku's voice was half question, half greeting. He didn't expect an answer and he didn't get one. Matt proceeded to load five sheets of plate iron on his wagon, then three dozen oak timbers. But what surprised Pikku most of all was what came out of the baggage car—a ship's bell! What did Matti want with a ship's bell?

Soon the rumours spread to every household on the Coteau. Matt Inhonen was building a ship—on his farm, in that deep valley. What could he possibly do with a ship that far from the river? He must be crazy.

Urho and Fred talked Lempi into going with them. She was curious. Maybe she should take some *pulla* for Matt, but she was sure he would refuse it and that would be an embarrassment for both of them. The saskatoons were ready but she knew that the boys wouldn't stop long enough to pick, so there was no need to bring a pail with her. They'd have to walk once they got to the valley. She put on a second pair of heavy stockings to make walking through the shrubs easier on her legs.

The first thing they noticed was the sound: clang, clang, clang.... They saw far below, Matt wielding a sledge hammer, and the sound came on the upswing, clang, clang, clang, clang. He stood beside a smoking forge. Behind him they could see the beginnings of two curved frames, and a small cabin.

"What do you think it is, Lempi?" Urho asked. "Do you think it is a ship?"

"A ship?" Fred said. "Do you think it is a ship? What good is a ship down there? We are fifteen miles from the river, a shallow river at that."

Lempi rubbed her heavy forearm with her hand. "Pikku says it is a ship. Matt Inhonen will build it in three pieces, including the little cabin he lives in already. Pikku says Matt will raft these pieces some springtime on high water to the Hudson's Bay."

"What else did Pikku say?"

"He said that Inhonen doesn't talk, but he has a map pencilled on the ceiling of his cabin. It shows Hudson's Bay, and Finland, and he has drawn beside the map a big chart of the stars in the sky. That is what Pikku says."

Fred helped Lempi down from the wagon and Urho led the horse to a saskatoon bluff where he tied it in the shade. They walked down into the valley where, in steep places, Urho held Lempi by the elbow. Halfway down the hill they stopped by a stone structure, a shed started for some purpose but left unfinished. From there they watched. Inhonen looked up at them only once. He pumped the bellows of his forge, heated iron plate, then hammered, heated again, pumped the bellows, lifted out the red hot iron and hammered again.

For a long time they watched. Lempi thought of the old Finnish legends. How stubborn those gods were. How they could make things. To build a boat all that *Väinämöinen* had to do was sing his magic. *Ilmarinen* had to work. This one below is *Illmarinen*, Lempi thought. At his forge *Ilmarinen* built the pillar on which the world rests. *Ilmarinen* built the *Sampo*. This ship business reminded her of *Kalevala*. This Inhonen reminded her of those heroes driven by who knows what.

Matt set his hammer down, and walked to the slough several yards from his cabin. In the slough they could see planks weighted down with rocks in the water. That was the way the men in Finland bent wood to build their boats, Lempi thought. At the slough Matt filled a tin can with water, got coffee from his cabin, then set the can to boil on the forge. He stirred the coffee as it boiled. Finally he looked up at Lempi and the boys, blinked repeatedly, then jerked his head, beckoning them. The coffee was bitter, and Fred wished he had brought lump sugar. He dared not ask Matt for sugar. Fred was close to bursting with curiosity. He knew that Urho would never ask about anyone else's business, and as for Lempi, it was good enough that she came along. Fred had to find out about the boat. Imagine, a boat in this valley... right out of the bible—Noah's ark.

"You have this frame," Fred said, as he ran his hands along the oak boards.

Matt mumbled slowly. "Ya, that is start for the keel, ship's bottom, ballast, you know, ballast? For weight? So the boat doesn't tip in the rough water?"

Fred nodded. He bit his lip. He could hold his curiosity no longer. "Why do you build this ship?"

The creases in Matt's forehead deepened. He said nothing, and Lempi knew it was time to go. He blames himself, Lempi thought, for Ruth's death. He hammers at the iron to pound at his guilt. He will hammer till he dies.

Somehow it is that every Finn must build a ship, not the biggest, not the smallest, and it is no one's business, only his. He tells nobody. It is for Swedes to brag, Lempi thought. Only a Finn would build a ship in a dry valley so he would have to drag it to the water. Who else could manage such a feat? Who could have the patience, the strength, the will? Why?

He lets no one know how urgent his mission is, how it eats at him. He takes his time, works as if it is nothing. Pikku says Matt paints the wood for his ship with blood from his horses.

Lempi looked through the smoke curling up from the forge towards the eastern ridge of the valley, rubbing her fingers. He will slave at his impossible ship forever.

Matt spoke. "I build my ship." His eyebrow twitched

and the skin tightened on his jaw. He placed his hand on the smooth bend of an oak rib. "I build alone." He picked up his hammer.

Lempi motioned for the boys to leave. They walked away, and she followed. Fred looked back once, then all three climbed slowly to the top of the valley.

Chapter Twelve

Thus he got the sword he wanted,
The most excellent of blades,
And he cut down all the nation
And destroyed the host of Unto;
Burned the homestead down to ashes,
Smouldering down to very cinders,
Leaving only hearthstones standing
And the rowan in the farmyard.

Kalevala, Runo 36

Ya, that Matti is a hermit, Lempi thought. Better he is a hermit than a Red. If only Urho and Sirkku would quit all that communist nonsense. It scared Lempi when the policemen came three or four times a year, driving into the yard, asking them questions. At least Lempi didn't speak English, that was good. But there was so much of this red business, more and more socialist refugees coming from Finland. And then of all things, Otto Jukola coming to Dunblane. Imagine, all the way from that hunting lodge in Finland, here to Dunblane.

Maybe I could go to town and visit at his barbershop some Saturday—I could tell him how Senja died. He'd want to know about his sister. But how can I go to town, to the barbershop—the women don't go to the barbershop, and Urho and Sirkku will have nothing to do with their Uncle Otto. Sirkku has Otto's letter. *Voi, voi,* I should have burned the letter before she got her hands on it—all this gossip she writes in the *Työmies.*

On Sunday while Lempi was at Tenho's place for church, and Urho had skied to the hall to light the fire for the YCL meeting,

Sirkku was home alone, preparing to write her news. The kitchen was filled with the aroma of boiling coffee. She stirred it, then moved the pot to the back of the stove. She turned around and felt the fire's heat sink into her skin—her buttocks and legs. She filled her cup and walked to the window.

Sunlight glinted on snowflakes like twinkling stars tumbling in the stillness. The air was so quiet that the snow had built little mounds, like bunkers on the top of the fence-posts. In front of the oat-bin door a prairie chicken scratched at the snow. Sirkku grabbed her arms tight across her chest and shivered, reaching for her sweater on the back of the chair. She rummaged in her pocket for the letter, a three-year-old letter written by Otto Jukola. Otto had mailed the letter from Finland to her mother, but it arrived months after she was dead. Sirkku had read it many times. She sat at the table and read it again.

Dear Sister Senja,
The Civil War is over. The Red devils
have been beaten....

"Red devils!" she thought. Thousands of young workers, that's all. Can Finland belong only to the rich? At youth club meetings when Sirkku was thirteen, Hilja Mukari instructed them on the events of this war. Sirkku knew the background of the struggle. One hundred thousand 'landless ones'—children of those poor peasants, working for the Russian Czar during the Imperialist War—digging the ditches around Helsinki—protecting the city from the Kaiser.

And then Revolution in St. Petersburg—the Bolsheviks—Russia out of the war—the 'landless ones' in Helsinki—no more jobs.

'Red Guards'—these landless youngsters—joined with Social Democrats. Like Bolsheviks they seized the power in Finland—a Red Finland.

She remembered how excited Hilja was, then how dejected when the coup failed. The Jääkari were too strong, Mannerheim, the 'White Guards,' had crushed the Red brothers and sisters during those few bitter months in 1918. Otto's letter bragged about what followed this defeat:

> *At the lodge we have in the compound,*
> *five thousand prisoners. I am in charge*
> *of discipline. They were a defiant lot*
> *at the beginning, and we had to show*
> *them who was in charge. My superiors*
> *ordered me to shoot every tenth*
> *prisoner. Each day one hundred men*
> *were selected to draw lots from*
> *a bucket. In it were ten red pellets.*

"Dirty butchers!" Sirkku said, and she nibbled on her thumbnail.

She had clipped out a picture from the previous week's *Työmies,* a photograph someone had taken in one of those camps. On a snow-covered lake a soldier, wearing a greatcoat and holding a rifle, looked down at his feet where there were several bundles on the ice—about ten, as far as she could make out—bundles like sacks of potatoes. The bodies of the dead.

> *I had a scare the other day. In the line*
> *of one hundred men, I saw our brother,*
> *Emil. I hadn't known he was a Red. I*
> *can only thank God that our brother*
> *drew a black pellet.*

Isn't that just like those 'white butchers'! Like Hilja Mukari says: "Otto is a pawn. They use him as a fist to beat hunger out of men's bellies and sense from their heads!"

> *I thought much about it. When things*
> *are settled here, I am going to*
> *emigrate. I have had unhappiness—*
> *I didn't tell you—while I was fighting*
> *for my country, my wife ran off*

with some godless Red traitor...

"And now," she said, "my Uncle Otto, his hands soiled with workers' blood, is a barber in Dunblane."

Sirkku shook her head.

She massaged her neck, rubbed her cheekbones, wet her lips, rotated her shoulders, drew them back and swung her arms wide. She adjusted the paper in the roller and began typing:

> *We have a certain countryman who has*
> *arrived in our district. His name is*
> *Otto Jukola.*
> *This White Finn has bragged that after*
> *the Finnish Civil War, how he dared send*
> *eighteen Reds to Abraham's lap. What a*
> *hero, who takes the life of an unarmed*
> *worker. For such a hero, Blood General*
> *Mannerheim gave a spruce twig for his*
> *lapel, and a passport to Canada, thus*
> *bribing his heroes. That's all they really*
> *deserve—a dry spruce twig....*

The following morning Sirkku went to Dunblane to mail her report, and Otto Jukola spotted her from the barbershop window.

"That's her, my niece!" Otto said, placing his hand on the shoulder of Hamilton Pringle, owner of the General Store, and town mayor. The barber leaned to Pringle's ear. "She just came from your store, and she's going into the post office."

The mayor stared out the window. "Not bad looking. Filled out, that's for sure. Nice hitch to her walk."

"She is a communist," Otto whispered.

"Oh?" The Englishman picked clippings of hair from his neck. "Pretty thing like that?" He studied the mirror in front of him. "Maybe you should cut a little more from the top, Otto. Your niece, eh? She doesn't look like a communist.... Say, is it right that all you Finns carry knives?"

"Oh, no, no, not me. But the Reds—yes, they are devils."

Hamilton Pringle stroked his cheek several times. "I think maybe you should give me a shave too, Otto."

The barber lathered Pringle's face, and began stropping his razor. The store owner laid his head back and closed his eyes. "Do you think a young lass like your niece could be dangerous?" he said.

"Oh, yes, it is especially the young ones. I saw what they tried in Finland. We put a stop to that, but you never know what can happen here." The lather peeled off in a fluffy roll from Hamilton Pringle's throat, and Otto wiped the razor with his towel. "The Red Finns are having a celebration at their hall this summer—the Mid-summer Festival, a big sportsday, political speeches, plays, and dancing. It is their biggest event of the year."

"I wonder," Hamilton said, turning to the window, careful not to disturb the lather on his face. "Do you think the police should check it out?"

With the razor in his hand, Otto Jukola looked at his customer, and raising his eyebrows and pursing his lips, he shrugged, then nodded.

Chapter Thirteen

This is how the lucky knew it,
How an utter stranger learned it
That the girl-child had grown up,
Had attained her maidenhood:
'Well, well, how now, my little maid!
Didn't I always tell you, warn you
Not to cuckoo in the fir groves
Nor to sing along the valleys,
Not to show your neck so archly
Nor the whiteness of your arms,
Not the fullness of your bosom
Nor any other charm of body.'

Kalevala, Runo 19

Lempi grumbled. The cookstove was hot and so was she. The stove had to be hot to heat the irons because that pest Pikku Juntinen wanted his trousers pressed for tomorrow's Midsummer Festival. She grumbled because to iron pants for this Festival was devil's work. Ah, but what could she do? Pikku always came to help when he was needed. Even when he wasn't needed. She worried about Urho and Sirkku. They were growing up, and more and more they went to these gatherings at the devil's hall. And more young ones kept coming from Finland, from the wars—Reds. They had been beaten, and now they came here. All Sirkku can talk about is this Mid-summer Festival—the biggest crowd ever they will have, she says. Sirkku is secretary of the Young Communist League, and there she is at the hall every Saturday morning planning the Festival program with Hilja Mukari, and practising for a play, when she should be cleaning house. It wouldn't be so bad if it was just Sirkku, but what will brother Tenho think when he finds out that Eva came for sauna tonight just so she can go to the Festival with Sirkku? Ya, what are they doing in that sauna for so long? Are they going to cook themselves?

Eva and Sirkku sat on a lower bench in the sauna, now and then splashing cool water on one another from a basin between them, talking about their plans for the next day. The two of them were oblivious to the glistening of their wet bodies. Sirkku, with fair hair, high cheek-bones, and her mother's graceful fullness of body, displayed more confidence than the timid Eva. Sirkku sat forward on the bench, scrubbing her thighs with a brush. Eva leaned back, her long dark hair trailing on her arms, her neck against the edge of the top bench. Eva had never been to a Mid-summer Festival.

"I like your hair," she said. "Mother won't let me cut mine."

Sirkku stopped her scrubbing, and poured the water from the basin onto her lap. She turned to Eva and said, "At our Young Communist League meeting last Sunday we discussed the role of women in the Class Struggle. That is why I cut my hair short."

"What do you mean?" Eva asked.

"As long as men look at women as playthings, we are the oppressed class," she said.

Eva looked at Sirkku's feet, her thighs, slim waist and firm breasts, her wet body gleaming darkly in the semi-darkness of the sauna. Sirkku was silly, cutting her hair for the class struggle. What would she think of next?

In the morning the girls dressed quickly. In no time they were sitting in the back of Pikku Juntinen's 1922 Ford truck, their picnic baskets, adorned with red and yellow ribbons, held on their laps.

They shared the truckbox with Pikku's base drum, fifteen cases of pop, and several large chunks of ice buried in wet sawdust.

A group of eight young men and women walked along the road on their way to the hall. Pikku stopped and they climbed into the box. The truck passed several families on horse-drawn wagons, all on their way to the festival.

Puffs of dust from the tires hung in the air behind the truck, and along the roadside and in the pastures gophers stood alert. Foolish gophers, the young ones were afraid of nothing. Everybody goes to the hall but the church people, Eva thought. Father says the Mid-summer Festival is the Devil's work. And that Lempi. After sauna last night she told us that at one place in Finland, the singing of Russian dance songs and the shouting of the 'Evil One' was said to come from under the floor of the dance hall.

Eva didn't care what her father or Lempi thought—not today.

Several Model A's and a dozen or so wagons were already on the grounds. Pikku parked beside a truck loaded with freshly-cut poplar branches. One man was lifting the leafy boughs and handing them to another man fashioning a roof on the concession stand. With an axe Pikku broke up chunks of his ice in a watering trough and the girls helped with the pop. The bottles clinked musically against each other.

Then Pikku took his drum from the truck and called the rest of the band members to get ready for the parade. Urho and Fred appeared on the hall steps unfurling a huge red banner. People marched five or six abreast around the grounds, Urho and Fred with the banner, and Pikku with his drum, leading the procession. Sirkku and Eva joined the parade under the *New Dawn Drama Club* banner. Behind her, Eva could see many other flags—the *Young Pioneers, New Dawn Athletic Club, Young Communist League, Socialist Women's Club*. Eva had a glimpse of Hilja Mukari munching on a hot dog, marching proudly under the *Coteau Hill Finnish Socialist Women's Organization*. The banners bounced above the heads of the line of people singing, and the band played *Internationale,* to the beat of Pikku's drum. Old men marched, young women carrying infants, with children tugging at their skirts. Grandmothers walked. Men in ball uniforms. Boys running in and out of the line, pinching the girls. Hundreds were in the parade.

In spite of the excitement of the races (she herself had won the sixty-yard dash) and the excitement of watching Urho's ball game, Eva worried all day about the supper. Sirkku had said there'd be a basket lunch auction. Eva didn't say anything, but secretly she wished that it would be Sirkku's brother who would buy hers. She wondered if anybody knew that she liked Urho?

She and Sirkku had prepared their baskets the night before. They had taken a few slices of Lempi's *pulla*. No one made coffee bread as good as Lempi. Would Lempi know it was gone? She didn't approve of them going to the festival. How many times had she said that the festival was the Devil's work? What would Lempi think if she knew that her *pulla* was at the festival?

That stupid Fred at the auction! The women set their baskets on the tables outside the hall. Fred knew which was Eva's basket; no names were on them, but everybody knew. The boys whispered the names around. They knew what they were bidding on. Fred kept upping Urho's bid. Eva could have killed him. How high would Urho go? Eva didn't think he would go as high as he did: nine dollars, the highest price for any basket!

By themselves at last Urho and Eva left the grounds and went to the open prairie for their picnic. The day was just beginning to cool off. They walked over a hill, and down into a dip to the edge of a patch of buckbrush mixed with prairie rose bushes.

Eva pulled at a rose, then quickly raised her hand to her mouth, and sucking her finger, tried to draw out a tiny thorn with her teeth. Urho set the basket down and, with his knife, cut flowers and arranged a small bouquet for Eva.

"Let's eat here," she said, spreading a blanket. Opening the wicker basket she began carefully laying things out: plates, knives and forks, melted butter, salt and pepper shakers, three hard-boiled eggs, a quart sealer of jellied chicken, also melted, a bowl of radishes, leaf lettuce, prune tarts, four slices of Lempi's *pulla*, and two bottles of strawberry soda-pop. She handed Urho the sealer to open. Peeling eggshells and buttering the *pulla,* Eva couldn't remember ever being so happy.

Urho speared a chicken leg from the jar and began eating. Eva handed him a peeled egg.

"Look," Urho said, "a weasel." It stood on its hind legs, beside a pile of small rocks on a side-hill about fifty yards away, watching them. For a moment it didn't move, and then quickly its body looped, and it glided over the ground like a water droplet trickling down a window-pane. It stood again, jumped into the air, then vanished between the rocks.

"The prairie is full of surprises," Urho said. "You know, my mother loved the prairie. She used to say that the heart of the land here is not in one place, but everywhere. Out here it hides, and we are lucky when we see things like that weasel."

"Wouldn't it be something," Eva said, hugging her knees, "if a moment could last forever?"

The sun was half a disk on the horizon, then slowly and without notice it dropped from sight. The Coteau spread itself in all directions, dipping and rising, like a bulging pie crust. The horizon was starting to fuzz and dim, except for the northwest segment, where the peach-glow remnants of the sun's light showed the clear and bumpy line of the Coteau. A homestead shack stood out on the line, cleanly black, simple, against the peach sky. Clouds formed by the heat in the late afternoon had now mostly disappeared, and what remained were flat purple wisps.

"It is so quiet," Eva said. "At Mid-summer in Finland people our age stay up all night."

"Where did you hear that?"

"From Lempi. She told me the Finns light huge bonfires. In pagan times they believed that the solstice gave birth to new life."

Urho touched Eva's bare arm. She shivered as he leaned forward and kissed her on the lips. He brushed a rose petal lightly against her cheek and ran his finger along her neck. Distant shouts came from the direction of the hall.

"Pikku must have arrived with the ice-cream," Urho said. "We better hurry if we don't want to miss it." Eva quickly packed the dishes, shook and folded the blanket, stuffed it into the wicker basket, and they ran, laughing, across the prairie to the fairgrounds.

Sunburnt girls and boys crowded around the concession, running back and forth, begging their fathers for nickels. Pikku was standing in the booth with his hands in his pockets, while in front of him a fat woman held three empty cones in her hand and rapidly scooped ice-cream from the cardboard tub in the horse-trough.

"Ya! Urho! Buy your girlfriend an ice-cream." Pikku yelled like an auctioneer, laughing to the crowd. The woman filled the cones, handed them to the children, while Pikku stood licking a double-decker, the ice-cream dripping onto his hand.

After the tubs were emptied, after the mothers, wives, and girlfriends had packed away their picnic blankets and dishes, the crowd moved into the hall. Eva noticed the hardwood floor—a big floor for dancing. Was Lempi's Devil under that floor? Gold letters were sewn on the stage curtains—*Workers of the World Unite; You Have Nothing to Lose but Your Chains*. Sirkku and the girls in the Young Communist league had sewn them.

Above the stage hung a portrait of a bald-headed man, and beside that picture was the red banner Urho and Fred had carried that morning.

"Who is that in the picture?" Eva asked Urho. Hilja Mukari, seated in the row behind them, leaned forward. "That is the Great Lenin."

Urho pointed to the stage door. "The Young Pioneers are going to sing in English," he said. Seven girls and three boys, smartly dressed in white shirts with red scarfs tied at their necks, marched to the stage.

"Pikku wanted the song in Finn," Urho said.

Hilja leaned forward again. "Ah, that old Pikku, he will just have to accept it. If we are to establish the international brotherhood of workers, we can't do it talking only Finn."

Sirkku struck a loud chord on the piano, and the audience stood facing the ten Young Pioneers. She led the singing of *The Red Flag* :

> *The people's flag is deepest red,*
> *It shrouded oft our martyred dead,*
> *And ere their limbs grew stiff and cold,*
> *Their heart's blood dyed its ev'ry fold.*

Hilja Mukari walked to the front and spoke in Finn. She talked for two hours, first about club matters—memberships and subscriptions for *Työmies*. Then she spoke about famine relief for the Red Finns who had fled east from Finland to Karelia in the new Soviet Union. These people needed tools: axes, cross-cut saws, grub-hoes, rope. They needed cattle, engines, gasoline, seeds. They needed dishes and food—immediately.

Her speech was interrupted by the entrance of two policemen. One was tall and thin, the other, stocky. Pikku confronted them at the door, speaking in his slow musical manner, in Finn. A policeman asked him to speak English. Pikku, scratching his head and puffing on his cigarette, beckoned for Urho.

"What is the trouble?" Urho said.

The stocky policeman answered. "The Red Flag over the stage, and that picture, cannot be displayed in a Canadian hall, unless the Union Jack and a portrait of King George the Fifth is prominently mounted above them. In the name of the King, I am ordering you to stop these proceedings, and disperse."

Hilja joined the discussion.

"Ya," she said, "but we are having a dance. What can we tell the people?"

"Tell them it's five minutes until midnight. It is against the law to hold dances on Sunday." The policemen gave them twenty minutes to clear the hall.

Chapter Fourteen

Only yesterday a slave,
Very early in the morning
Furrowed out a field of adders,
Turning up a snaky acre,
When the ploughshare raised a chest lid
Which disclosed a hoard of coins
Heaped in hundreds, stacked in thousands.

Kalevala, Runo 12

Every year in late summer when the saskatoons were ripe, Lempi took a long walk to the hillsides of Matt Inhonen's valley. Each year she saw Matt's progress on the building of his ship. On this day he pounded on the iron steam boilers, cold-welding the seams. She wondered whose dream was crazier— the shipbuilder's, or her grandson's dream of revolution? Tenho told her he had heard the men laughing at the barber-shop. They said that Urho, Sirkku, his own Fred, that all of them were red hot.

Five years ago Urho and Eva were married—May Day, 1925. Sirkku had been so excited planning her brother's wedding for May Day, as if it were Christmas.

In this new country the young people turn their backs to God, and Lempi could see how this faithlessness grieved Tenho. His health had been failing ever since Ruth died from the influenza. Ya, Lempi thought, so much sorrow there has been for Tenho. Eva's marriage was simply one more sorrow.

The berries were dry and shrivelled like currants, not plump and juicy like last year. She heard the ping of each berry hit the bottom of her milk pail, and far below at the bottom of the valley, she heard the ringing blows of Matti's hammer.

What will the future bring for Urho and Eva? Lempi helped bring their son Paul into the world. The doctor in Dunblane handled most of the maternities in the district now, but he had been away on business to Regina. Eva delivered the baby in the bedroom. Lempi wondered if it was these modern doctors who talked the young women out of birthing in the sauna. She thought the sauna would have quickened the baby's delivery, but who could say? One thing she knew for sure— cleaning up the bed was ten times more work than the old way. Lempi washed the baby in the old way, a little salt in the water to toughen him, and then gave him to his mother. Watching Eva nurse the child reminded Lempi of herself at age fourteen, of Taisto's birth. The memory saddened her, but she was happy for Urho and Eva. In a moment of weakness, succumbing to the ancient superstition, she carried the placenta out of the house. Behind the barn where no one could see, she buried it under a rock.

Ya, Lempi thought, brother Tenho liked the name. Eva named her baby after Ruth's Paul. But a child's name will not bring Eva's parents to her. Unless she repents there must be this separation. Lempi knew—it had to be.

The milk pail was half-full of berries and Lempi moved to another bluff. Breathing fresh air and picking saskatoon berries relieved her depression. So many bad things had happened, so much unbelief, false beliefs. Each year more and more politics—could it be the world ending? Each year in these 1920's the light became dimmer, the world sank deeper into hell—ten steps into the blackened caves of *Tuonela*.

So much hatred in this country, hardening of hearts. Lempi knew what happened in the field southeast of Dunblane— a strange event. Bizarre, the English said.

Otto Jukola was involved, and home-brew, Pikku's home-brew. Urho said that minds were getting sick in Saskatchewan. She knew more and more that Urho wanted to leave the country—to go to Soviet Karelia.

Sirkku said nothing about the event in *Työmies*. Maybe it couldn't be talked about publicly, one of those things so horrible that it cannot be talked about. Anyway, nothing was said aloud, only whispers. For sure Otto Jukola didn't talk.

The scheme began on a quiet morning. Otto Jukola was sweeping the sidewalk in front of his barbershop, enjoying the warmth of the sun and the dusty smell of the sweepings.

"No haircuts yet this morning, Otto?" Hamilton Pringle called. "Why don't you drop that broom and come over a minute? I've got some things I want to ask you."

"I'll just finish up here, Mr. Pringle...." Otto stepped into his shop and propped his broom beside a dust-mop in a small closet by the entry. He hastened out the door, locked it, and crossed the street.

The floor of Pringle's General Store was freshly oiled, giving a sharp clean odour. Otto detected also the distinct aromatic sweetness of plug chewing tobacco and Copenhagen snuff, displayed in a case on the wall beside the clock.

Hamilton Pringle was on his haunches sorting through a bin of oranges, picking out the spoiled ones. He turned, and with one hand pressed to his knee, got to his feet. With a hooked knife he carefully removed rotten bananas from the stalk hanging above his head. He carried the garbage out back in a coal pail.

He came back in, straight to the cheese cutter, wiped his hands with a white apron, and cranked the big round of aged Ontario cheddar.

"Would you like a bit of cheese, Otto?"

The barber shook his head.

"You know, Otto, quite a few of the businessmen in town belong to this new club we have. At our last meeting we thought we might approach you about joining. You like to hear about it?"

Otto knew what Hamilton Pringle was referring to. He knew the Ku Klux Klan had organized in Dunblane, and suspected that the store owner was a member.

"Would you like to join the Klan, Otto?"

Otto hadn't ever heard of a Finn being asked to join.

The Klan was composed of English, Orangemen, secret people in the Masons.

Otto looked around, making sure they were alone. "Can I ask you a question, Mr. Pringle?" Hamilton nodded his head, biting into his cheese. "What is it you do? What do you stand for in this organization?"

"I'm glad you asked that, Otto. You see, it's mostly about patriotism—about the King, and the Union Jack. We believe in British Democracy—the English language, yes, and moral standards. We are against alcohol—the wide open prostitution in Moose Jaw—the Frenchmen trying to force their language on everybody—all those garlic-smelling bohunks coming into Canada as if they own it—and of course, Communism."

To Otto much of this made sense. He had fought the Red Menace in Finland, and was convinced that Canada's Mackenzie King government was not nearly enough aware of the threat of communism.

"How do I join?" he said.

"I'll take the fact that you are interested to the next meeting, Otto. Meanwhile, there is something for you to do. A kind of test. So we know for sure you have the right stuff in you."

"Ya?"

"You knew did you Otto, that Frank Templeton's daughter is in the family way?"

"Oh?" Otto was noncommittal.

"These things happen—Frank being the station agent— Jenni around all the time when the trains come in. All those travellers. Such a shame. And the girl so young, only fifteen." Hamilton's voice was quieter, more and more conspiratorial.

"What do you want me to do?" Otto asked.

"Anyway, we know who the man is—a traveller for Salada Tea—here tell he's a Finn come west from Port Arthur. Been coming to the store no more than a year or two. About six months ago he took the girl to one of those Finn hall dances, and he done it to her."

Otto remembered this salesman. In fact he had been in for a haircut the very day of the dance—asked him if anybody made home-brew in Dunblane. Otto fixed him up with a quart he'd got himself from Pikku Juntinen.

"How can I help, Mr. Pringle?"

"He's coming in on tomorrow night's train, Otto. We'll have a little reception for him out at the old Henley place—by the slough in the pasture. Do you think you can get him there?"

"Ya, I think so," Otto said.

The salesman stepped down from the passenger car and stood for a moment, resting his large black carrying case on the platform. He had delicate features: dark hair slicked back over his narrow forehead, a long, pointed nose, a tiny mouth, narrow shoulders, and small feet. Otto approached him, offered to carry his sample case, and asked if he knew when the Orange Crush soda-pop traveller was coming in from Saskatoon. The little man shrugged his shoulders. Said he didn't know. Otto talked all the way to Jimmy Wong's cafe.

The place was empty except for Jimmy and two old men playing cards on the counter by the cash register. Otto bought coffee and sat with the salesman at a back booth where it was darker. After their second cup of coffee, and the sales-man's third cigarette was butted into the ashtray, Otto produced a coke bottle containing a small measure of Pikku Juntinen's home-brew. He poured an ounce into the man's cup and told him if he wanted a gallon to take with him to Saskatoon, they could hike out to Otto's stash a mile southeast of town and get it.

It was already dark when the two of them set out on the road to Henley's pasture. The sky was clouded over and the salesman could barely see his shoes on the gravel.

"Are you sure that you know where we are going?" he asked.

"Just follow me—we cross into this ditch here. Wait, I'll hold up the wire—don't rip your pants on the fence. My stash is in a bluff about three hundred yards from here."

There was little sound but for the rumbling of frogs—a continuous rumbling from the slough somewhere ahead. The air was cool and still. Crickets chirped. "We are just about there now," Otto said. "Wait here. I'll get it."

The salesman was suddenly alone and it didn't bother him. But after a while he began to sense that he was waiting a long time. It seemed as if the frogs croaked louder, and then as these sounds continued, each cricket call one at a time became sharper and sharper, as if knifing the air into chunks.

He smelled gasoline, which he thought was strange, and then he sensed something ahead of him—and above—something that had been there all the time—a black form appearing in the blackness. Only when a light appeared behind it could he see it was a cross.

Then the lights came—another and another—at least a dozen lanterns swayed towards him, and he was surrounded by white-sheeted figures.

A light touched the black cross. Flames shot from it like two arms waving and a ghoulish head laughing. Men grabbed and pinned him to the ground. They stretched him out, spread-eagled, his hands and feet tied to railroad spikes pounded into the hard ground. A man stood over him. Lantern light reflected off the steel razor in his hand.

The salesman began screaming. "No! No! No!"

"Just a little treat for Jenni," the voice above him whispered.

The Klansman knelt between the splayed legs and cut open the seam at the man's crotch. With his hand he ripped apart the undershorts. Like a surgeon with his scalpel in one hand, he lifted the testicles with the other, the flabby skin was like the pebbled crop of a plucked chicken.

The delicate man screamed and screamed through the clustered lanterns, the sound echoing beyond the spiralling halo of the cross.

Otto watched from behind the trees. His hands and knees were wet, sunk into the slough bog. He vomited.

Chapter Fifteen

Then the winds began to blow,
Vehement storms to rage with fury.
High the west wind lashed the water,
And the southwest with more fury;
Even stronger blew the south wind,
While the east wind whistled madly;
Awesomely the southeast howling,
And the north wind weirdly wailing.

Kalevala, Runo 42

Lempi's grandson Paul was on his knees by a rockpile, scooping at an anthill with an old shingle. The ants crawled up the wood, carting their eggs. Lempi sat on a big rock watching the loose dirt boiling with ants, and then she felt something on her leg, not an ant—something bigger, a grasshopper. It had jumped on her lap and then to her knee. She felt the grip of its legs through her dress. As she picked up the grasshopper, one of its back legs arched awkwardly to the side, gripping like a pincer on her finger. It turned its head, as if eyeing her, and it spit a green stain on her thumbnail.

Three crop failures. Look at this burnt-up wheatfield, nothing left even for the cows. They've been scrounging a month already and all that's left is Russian thistle—tumbleweeds. Like fat porcupines, the thistles look like ten thousand porcupines all over the field.

Ya, so who can blame Urho for wanting to go to Karelia. Anyway, for one thing, it won't be dry like this. Eva won't have all this dirt blowing into the house—the cupboards full of dirt. Dirt on the wash hanging on the clothes-line. But of all places, why Karelia? The grasshoppers should go, but why do the young people go? They will have no food to put in the cupboards, if even they have cupboards. Sirkku is there, and Fred, gone a year already. Some are coming back, but not Sirkku. She won't come back.

Pikku and Urho have made a deal. They built a new fence. Pikku is bringing his cattle and horses to keep with ours. I will have Pikku at the doorstep morning and night. Lempi shook her head. That's enough worrying about this Karelia. She dropped the grasshopper on the anthill and listened to the men talking by the fence.

"Ya," Pikku said, his voice in its slow high-pitched twang, "I don't think even the Anderson government can make it rain." He tossed his hammer on the wagon, rubbed his sweating forehead with his cap, scratched his head, and then reaching into his pocket, he drew out a red polkadot handkerchief and wiped around his neck. He grabbed the jug of water from under the wagon and sat down. "I will keep my cattle at your place, Urho. That's a good idea. My well is dry, and maybe I can help keep the banker away. For sure the farmers have a fight on their hands." Pikku rolled a cigarette, struck a match on the iron band of the wagon wheel. "How did you make out with the Conservative Premier Anderson?"

"Premier! I can think of a better name. He wouldn't even come out on the steps to meet our delegation."

"Ya, Anderson. Do you remember the day you started school, Urho?"

"The 'kiss my ass' business? How could I forget?"

"In those years Anderson was in charge of educating immigrants. The Conservatives wanted us singing in English—God Save the King, and the sooner the better."

"I wrote him a letter," Urho said. "Asked him for some money. The English papers boasted that if a red farmer wanted to go to Russia, Anderson would pay the ticket. I am still waiting for an answer."

Pikku blew smoke from the side of his mouth, rolling the cigarette around on his lips. "I tell you something, Urho— what Hilja Mukari says. In the bible there is a verse—*the spirit indeed is willing, but the flesh is weak.* The conservatives rule by this passage, Hilja says—blame sin for all the troubles—a family starves because of its sins. God should know better. The rich rob the poor and blame the devil."

He stood, pulling at his trousers. "Let me quote you the bible according to Hilja: 'The flesh is willing, but the mind is weak.' The capitalist wants strong backs and weak minds to do his work. I remember what Matti used to say. Matti would say that the capitalist wants the workers to have less sense than a mule. Ya, that's right, when a mule is overloaded he doesn't pray to God to relieve him—he kicks like hell."

Lempi listened but didn't look their way. There was no point to argue with Pikku. How many times has he told that mule story? She looked out to the fields, saw the dust, the tumbleweeds rolling. She closed her eyes and heard the laments—*then the winds began to blow, vehement storms to rage with fury, awesomely the southeast howling, and the north wind weirdly wailing.*

Pikku continued. "We have been spoiled, playing at revolution, child's games, ever since we came here—not like the mines. Here our revolution centres on whether or not to sing God Save the King at a Mid-summer Festival. But maybe now with this drought it will be different. Nineteen cent wheat. The revolution comes."

"Ya, you think so Pikku? I wonder? I wonder if the people have the guts to stand up? No Pikku, I don't think so." Urho kicked dirt and it flew with the wind. "I will go to Karelia, be a part of a great achievement there—the Five-Year Plan in Soviet Karelia needs my farming skills."

The wind was gaining strength more and more, and Lempi sensed that the earth was angry. She held the boy close to her side. The wind chases like Louhi chased when the heroes stole the *Sampo*—the ugly bird screaming down from the sky in pursuit of *Väinämöinen.* The *Sampo* will be smashed. Dead Russian Thistles began breaking loose from the ground, rolling, slowly at first, hesitating, snagging now and then on the yellow sticks of straw. But when they reached the summerfallow, they raced, and soon they raced crazily, driven by the demon wind. Tumbleweeds skimmed across the fallow in straight lines, skilled in their racing, kicking dust with each hit at the earth. Lop-sided tumbleweeds jerked from side to side in a frantic dance, unsure of themselves, stopping now and then for balance. A long-stemmed tumbleweed vaulted, bounced on its stem in a wild leap. Two round tumbleweeds stuck together. They made oblong lurches into the air as if the giant wind had thrown them like mated dogs in a tangle.

It was a fleeing army of tumbleweeds. Like Cossacks on the Steppes the Russian Thistles spread in a random fleeting jumble across the field. As far as she could see in the mounting dust, the tumbleweeds raced. They raced like antelope and rabbits, as if panic-crazed, running from a prairie fire. They raced from no set starting line to a million places. Then Lempi heard Pikku's voice beneath the wind, heard him tell Urho....

"Ya," he said, lifting his cap, and wiping dust from his eyes with his handkerchief. "If I was a young man, I would go to Karelia."

Chapter Sixteen

"Goodbye now, my good father!
Will you mourn for me my father,
When you hear that I am dead
And have vanished from the nation,
Have departed from the clan?"

Kalevala, Runo 36

In 1931 the snow came in early November and stayed. At least Pikku was happy—the Russian thistles weren't blowing any more. The Sunday before last when Lempi was at Tenho's place for church, the fence along his road was a long brown clump of tumbleweeds as high as her shoulder. Now this fence was banked even higher, but it was a bank of snow, and the weeds were coated in white tinsel like Christmas trees.

She knew her brother Tenho was aware that Urho and Eva had already booked passage for Karelia, but he would expect Lempi to talk to him about the foolishness of it all. He wouldn't try to change Urho's mind. Tenho would never make such a bold attempt, and Urho wouldn't change his mind anyway, with or without Tenho's urging. Lempi understood these Finnish ways, and accepted them, even sometimes laughed at how silently stubborn her people could be. But anyway, she and her brother Tenho would want time together, contemplating, pondering the young couple's decision.

Lempi considered that if Urho and Eva wanted to emigrate it was none of her business, and she wouldn't interfere. She would have been more than willing to tell them what she knew about Karelia—how hard it would be to live—Lempi had been there, long ago with her father, and then she had been there that time at Taisto and Senja's wedding—but Urho would never ask her about what it would be like to live there, and if he wouldn't, neither would Eva. It was not in the nature of a Finn to pry.

When Lempi got to the farm, Tenho was by the well pumping water, his black Percheron standing beside him, its head lowered into the icy trough. Tenho frowned at his visitor, and then he smiled and shook his head, his saddened eyes holding a trace of their former gleam, his look suggesting to her that an old woman was foolish to be walking this far. Tenho led his horse to its stall in the barn, and then came out, brushing his few white wisps of hair to the side of his head with his fingers, extending his hand.

"Ya, God's Peace, Lempi. Come to the house—there is coffee."

Tenho hung his sister's coat on a hook in the porch, and pulled chairs from the kitchen table. "Maria is sleeping," he said. "She has a chill from this weather. It is too early for the winter, don't you think so, Lempi?" She nodded, sat, smoothing her dress with her hands.

The two of them remained silent a long while, listening to the coffee pot gurgling, the air puffing at the tin flap in the stovepipe vent, the pendulum wall-clock ticking back and forth. After a while Tenho poured coffee, and they sat some more. Finally Lempi sighed, pulled at her little finger, brushed her thumb across the back of her puffy hand.

"Pikku takes them to the train on Friday," she said.

Tenho looked at her, saying nothing, and then he reached for his bible on the table. He leafed the pages randomly back and forth as was his way, and then as if with God's help, the page was opened to him. He placed the bible on his lap, caressing the page with his shaking hand.

"I am only a mortal being, Lempi, full of weaknesses and shortcomings. In this matter we can only call on the Lord's help, and beg for grace."

He said this as if somehow he had failed in his duties as a parent, and Lempi wondered if this was where she differed from her brother. She accepted her grandson as he was. Maybe because Tenho was a man, he felt compelled to have his step-daughter believe as he believed, and would accept nothing else.

Daughters of Jerusalem, weep not for me,
but weep for yourselves, and for your
children. For behold, the days are coming,
in the which they shall say, Blessed are
the barren, and the wombs that never bare,
and the paps which never gave suck. Then
shall they begin to say to the mountains,
Fall on us; and to the hills, Cover us. For if
they do these things in a green tree, what
shall be done in the dry?

He did not comment on the passage, which was strange, because always he followed a bible verse with a sermon. But this one time he said nothing. Maybe he felt the passage needed no explaining, or maybe it was too painful.

Tenho closed the bible. He lifted it from his lap, set it down gently on the table, lowered his head, and shut his eyes. Lempi could see he would say nothing else—that for him the matter was settled.

"The train leaves Dunblane at night," Lempi said, "ten o'clock."

Three days later, Pikku and Lempi took the young family on the eight-mile sleigh ride to the train station. Eva sat under blankets on a pile of straw at the back of the box, Lempi beside her huddled in her buffalo coat. Urho and Pikku stood at the front, with little Pauli between them, holding the lines.

Ten thousand Finns, Lempi thought, that's what Otto Jukola said in town, ten thousand from America catching the Karelian Fever, going to some kind of new Workers' Republic north of Leningrad. Lempi saw these Russia journeys as a story from *Kalevala*, as if *Väinämöinen* and *Ilmarinen* were sailing off to the northland in quest of the *Sampo*. The bounties of the earth are born of the *Sampo*. These heroes sail off to steal the magic mill from its chained fortress. *Ilmarinen* cuts through nine iron chambers deep in *Louhi's* mountain, and then cuts loose the *Sampo's* roots. Lempi knew the *Sampo* would be smashed, the pieces scattered and lost, and the ten thousand Finns would flee, if they were able. The heroes in this sleigh-box go to *Louhi's* northland. The *Sampo* will be swept from the deck of *Väinämöinen's* ship and smashed to bits upon the water.

The hills by the road passing the Finn hall were silent, and the only sound came from the sleigh itself. Lempi listened to the metal tinklings of the chains, the snaps, and the buckles—the bells—the tugging harness leather, and the straining of the wooden sleigh box, like an old ship groaning—the swish of the runners over the snow, rasping on gravel where the wind had swept the snow away. She listened to the clopping hooves and muffling snorts of the big horses.

The Northern lights churned and leaped. The snow on the hills sparkled, and the horses' bells glittered, bouncing on the back-pads. She thought of fairies dancing on the hames in rhythm with the *jingle, jingle, jingle, jingle.*

"You know, Eva, I recall still from Finland the sleigh-ride when we crossed the ice bringing Senja to my place in Kuusamo." Eva nodded. "Ya," Lempi said, "peaceful like this night."

The sleigh came down from the hills and they could see the lights of Dunblane ahead of them on the flat. The train had arrived and was taking on water at the big tank.

By ten o'clock the family was on the train, looking out the window. The engine gave a jerk, then another, and another, slowly pulling the passenger car past the station, away from Lempi and Pikku on the platform. Eva had her head out the window. She waved, and then she saw him in the darkness. Tenho Maki was standing on his sledge by the freight shed. He waved his hand slowly, and Eva reached out as the train gained speed.

Chapter Seventeen

Said the dame of Pohjola:
"I did badly, very badly,
To have given any daughter,
Even when I sent the first one,
There to fall asleep so young,
Fade and wither in full flower—
Gave her to a wolfish mouth,
To the maw of growling bear."

There the maiden wept and wailed:
"Must I eat the famine bread,
Sour cranberries from the swamp,
Water arum from the ditches?
There this chicken will be lost,
I, this birdling, die untimely!"

Kalevala, Runo 38

North from Petroskoi, broken trees stuck out on each side of the road, their trunks ripped and twisted, roots upturned, as though something had smashed its way into the forest. A Komsomal labour brigade a year earlier had opened the trail to the Suna Collective Farm.

The truck filled with several families and their belongings passed a stumbling horse dragging a log. A wooden collar looped above the animal's shoulders, and a peasant clad in felt cap and boots, quilted pants and jacket, slouched behind on the snow-packed road. Urho watched, then slapping his shoulders with his mittened hands and stamping his feet, he turned to Paul.

"Yes, Pauli, I was a little boy like you when we left

Finland—country like this—snow, trees, dark at noon." The boy, covered in blankets, looked up from where he sat beside his mother on the pinewood chest. Urho continued. "Ya, we are not far from where I was born, maybe less than a hundred miles to the northwest."

For the last part of their journey a heavy snow fell, large floating snowflakes melting on their faces. Finally the truck reached the gate—two large trees stripped of their branches with a red star mounted above a cross-beam.

In this half-light, this half-darkness, all the broken things, what was unfinished, the things discarded—a tractor's seized engine garbaged in the trees, upturned stumps, a log house without a roof, a broken saw leaning against the wall—these things were softened by puffy blankets of snow.

A small band marched up the middle of the snow-covered street—two trumpets, a trombone, a french horn, a clarinet, and a drum like Pikku Juntinen's. They played *The Internationale,* and when the marching came to a halt, and the travellers had climbed down from the truckbox, Sirkku appeared.

"Welcome to Suna, welcome to the struggle of the working class." Snowflakes lit on the shoulders of her leather coat, skipped and fluttered down the arms. She hugged Eva, and wiped away tears, then getting back to business she pulled a ledger from her shoulder-bag. She called out names, and then continued with her official welcome, praising the people's arrival, giving information—how many cows on the farm, how many houses yet to build, how many thousand cords of pulpwood cut each month. But then Sirkku noticed the newcomers were tired from the journey, and she directed the band to take the families to the barracks. Soon she was alone with her brother Urho, Eva, and little Pauli.

"Urho, bring that chest...isn't that mother's old chest? Come, I show you where you live."

Urho looked about. Seven log houses sat in a row among trees. In a clearing further down he saw two silos (one of them unfinished) and a large barn. Three white-clad milkmaids walked across the clearing carrying wooden buckets.

"Come," Sirkku said. She led them to one of the buildings.

"Does Fred work on this farm?" Urho asked.

"No," Sirkku said. "He is somewhere near Kontupohja, on a logging brigade." She pulled at the strap of her shoulder-bag and shrugged. "Fred has too much vodka. Anyway, now that he is gone, the three of you can move in with me."

She took them into a building about the size of their old schoolhouse back home. Blankets were strung on rope to make four rooms, a family in each. "It's not as bad as it looks," Sirkku said, "but with just the one door there is not much privacy. The Canadians are coming faster than we can build, but if you brought extra blankets we can rope off a little sleeping area for me."

Later that evening they were able to find beds, and arranging the space the best they could, the family settled for the night. Sirkku talked from her blanketed alcove until it was almost morning.

"The movement is so vast," she told her brother. "It is difficult to fully grasp. Technically, we are at the primitive stage of development."

"I notice that," Urho said from his side of the blanket wall.

"The Five-Year Plan is a giant step forward to mechanization—that is why we are here."

Urho lay on his back and stared up at the black roof. He placed his hand on his sleeping wife's hip, heard the steady breathing of his son, and the snores from the other chambers. "So what do you think, Sirkku, are we going to make it work here?"

"Oh, of course it will not be easy. Some of the Finns feel cheated because of the shortage of food and living quarters. What makes it worse are people like Fred who don't know why they came in the first place. Oddly enough, it is those of us raised in Canada who manage the best—better than the native Finns coming from the civil war. I don't know why the Finns

—124—

complain. We have special stores where we can get meat, butter, cheese, flour, cereal grains, sugar, tea, eggs, tobacco..." She recited the items as if each commodity had a weighted value, like a diamond. "It is the Russians and the native Karelians who should complain."

Five weeks later, the day after New Year's, Urho was driving a truck from the engine shop to the dairy barn. So here we are, he thought, in the collective. No more pie-in-the-sky talk about a new dawn when the revolution comes. Here we live the revolution. It will take some getting used to. At home we had no money to buy things. Here there is nothing to buy. Even if the cows give milk, there are no cans to put it in. He stomped his feet on the floorboards. At least one thing is the same as Saskatchewan—the January cold.

Urho was to take milk to the corrective labour camp at Povenets. He could not imagine giving milk to class enemies, when it had to be rationed on their own farm. But this was only a one-time delivery, a bonus to a work team which for thirty consecutive days had exceeded its quota of earth removed from the canal excavation.

"Back the truck up to this door," the dairy worker said. He had a purple birthmark on his chin the size of a fifty-cent piece. "Climb into the box and I'll throw the milk up to you."

Urho couldn't believe it—oval blocks of frozen milk.

"We freeze it in washtubs," the worker said. "I see you get to drive the truck. American truck. American driver."

"Ya, I work in the engine shop. Everything from Henry Ford." Urho spoke with pride. "This truck was bought by the American Finnish Organization."

The dairyman kept throwing the slabs of white ice, "Eighty-three, eighty-four, eighty-five.... Have you got a smoke?" he said.

"Ya."

"American Tobacco?"

"Canadian," Urho said. He handed his tobacco pouch to the man. "Ogden's Fine Cut." He had brought thirty cans with him from Canada. "By the way, what do you know about the Povenets project?"

The worker sat on the loading dock and rolled a cigarette. "Ya," he said, "Part of the Five-Year Plan. The *White Sea-Baltic Stalin Canal* must be built in a short time, and we are spending not one kopeck on western machinery."

The dairy worker told Urho that the labour of one hundred thousand prisoners manned the canal project, mostly class enemies, Kulaks from Ukraine. "They sabotaged Collectivization," the worker said. "They tried to hide their stores of grain, buried it in the ground."

As Urho drove away from the barn, the worker waved and shouted, "On with the Five-Year Plan. Correction through labour will take us onward to the classless society."

The *Povenets Staircase* was to be a series of seven locks at the north end of Lake Onega. From a high embankment Urho looked out at the construction. The muted foggy light of mid-day polar winter, and the stretching rays of floodlights spread across the jagged hole. Countless boulders, and logs like a thousand games of Pick-Up-Sticks were scattered everywhere below, and the site was half-covered with snow. Here and there log tri-pods stuck up from the ground at odd angles, and a mass of people moved maggot-like over mounds and gouges. Urho saw a line of wheel-barrows immediately below him, coming up the embankment. A man pushed a wheelbarrow, and a woman wearing a silk dress and a ragged heavy woollen sweater pulled at the front with a hook. Far below in a pit several workers struggled with a boulder. They tried to lift it, roll it onto a platform placed on log rollers, but the boulder wouldn't budge. Other workers brought a net, secured it around the boulder, and over it they fashioned one of the tri-pod cranes. For more than an hour Urho watched them struggle with the boulder, rolling it onto the platform, pulling it all the way to the lock gates, and finally dumping it into the cribbing.

He was wasting time. Just one more cigarette and then he would look for the camp kitchen and unload the milk. Ya, his Ogden's tobacco. A bourgeois pleasure, he thought. Even before he left the Coteau, he'd been warned about the Russian Mahorka, and the information was true: the Mahorka did have the texture and taste of sawdust. The Ogden's was a treat. But the business of special privilege bothered him. He wondered about the social justice of having a special store for Finns. This was a strange arrangement, almost as if the Russians didn't expect them to carry the same weight as the natives. That morning before he left with the milk, he went to the Russian store for matches, and saw how bare the shelves were. A young woman had approached him at the counter. She was not bad looking, big in the chest, and she had pouting lips. She bent forward and slowly pulled her peasant blouse down from her shoulder. "Oh, big strong Americanski—I am woman for you." On the spot, she asked Urho to marry her. Then she could have the papers to buy food at the special store. When she lowered her blouse he could see that she wasn't starving yet. Her flesh still had its health. She was all right, that's for sure, he thought. But it saddened him to see how desperate the natives were. Urho wondered how this could possibly fit in with the concept of the new society and soviet man.

That evening Urho and Eva clung to each other quietly in their little cubicle. Snores resounded through their blanket walls.

"Remember the festival when you and I had the picnic?" Eva asked. "Remember when we saw the weasel—how it was a special moment?"

"Ya," Urho said, running his hand across her shoulder, twirling a strand of her long hair around his finger.

"We miss that here. There is no magic here."

"Ya," Urho said. "You are sick for home. But this is our new home, Eva—give it a chance. You know, I was reminded of something strange when I saw the canal today."

"Tell me," Eva said, snuggling closer.

"When I was a boy, Grandma Lempi told me stories— *Väinämöinen,* and the creation of the earth. The picture I have is the old man's mother floating on her back in the ocean. A duck laid seven eggs on her knee, and they hatched, falling into the water to begin the building of the world. The canal is like that ocean." Urho brushed the hair gently from her face and touched her cheek with his lips.

"You know, Eva, here we need to build the *Sampo.*

"*Sampo?*"

"When Lempi churned butter she would sing a song from the *Kalevala,* about the *Sampo.*

'One root into solid ground'

"And she would push the plunger down through the sloshing cream, and pull up:

'Another by a run of water
In the home hill grew a third.'

"It takes a long time to make butter. I would rock back and forth in her big chair listening while on and on she sang:

'The new Sampo then was grinding,
With its ciphered cover spinning;
Ground three binfuls every morning;

First a bin of things to eat,
Next a bin of things to sell,
Last a bin of things for home....'"

"You know, Urho, you should have dug the potatoes before it snowed."

"What potatoes?"

"At home. You were off at a meeting. You could have missed one meeting and dug the potatoes. The next morning it snowed. Do you think Lempi or Pikku might try and dig them, or will they be frozen?"

"For goodness sakes, Eva, why are you worried about potatoes thousands of miles away? Can't you forget about something that is done and gone with?" Urho tried to pull her to him but she turned the other way to lie flat on her back. She said nothing for a long time and Urho thought she was asleep. Then she spoke, quietly, more to herself than Urho.

"I worry about my brother," she said. "Where is Fred?"

Chapter Eighteen

He began to cut the salmon,
Slice the fish up with his knife.
Suddenly the beauty sprang
And it flipped into the sea
From the bottom of the red boat,
From the boat of Väinämöinen.

Kalevala, Runo 5

Lempi heard rumours about Fred Maki's fate. Was it true he hanged himself? Otto Jukola told Pikku in the barbershop that Fred was shot attempting an escape to Finland. Later they gossiped that he had starved to death in a labour camp. Families that came back said that was possible—it was easy enough to starve.

But Eva wrote in her letters that she didn't know what had happened to Fred, and probably never would. She and Lempi wrote to each other. Lempi's letters said *Your father's black horse died.... I should move to Dunblane, but I like to live alone here on the farm. Pikku has no water on his place so he keeps his cattle and team in the barn with my few cows. He is a pest like always, but all the same he is a big help since you've been gone.... Your mother and father are both very sick in the hospital together—they are not expected to last more than a year.... Pikku is upset that so many people are quitting from the Finnish Organization....*

Eva's letters from Karelia said *the store got in a supply of sugar—not the usual yellowed lumps of glass, but granular sugar, and my ration was enough to ice the cake for Pauli's seventh birthday.... Pauli has started grade 1 in the school for the Finnish children... Sirkku is showing an interest in the*

Russian doctor at Sunu.... Tell Mother and Father I am writing them—sometimes the letters get lost....

Ya, and Fred was lost. All his life he has been lost.

Kullervo pressed the haft against the heath,
turned the point against his breast, and
threw himself upon the point—there fulfilled
his destiny, chose dark death and met his doom.

Fred was in darkness. The path to heaven is straight and narrow, Tenho always said. When Fred was a boy he sneaked to the hall dances and Tenho whipped him. Did he hate Tenho for it?

Fred went to Russia not with Urho's sense of mission, nor with Sirkku's drive. He did not even know where Karelia was. Fred went to Russia because everyone else did, and if he was lucky, who knew, maybe he would find a home there.

At Sunu he moved in with Sirkku, but from their first night together everything went wrong. Whether he was too much in awe of both her body and spirit, or whether he was simply drenched with too much vodka, time and again he was unable to make love with her. After five months Sirkku kicked him out, saying that she was tired of nursing his headaches.

Shortly after he got wildly drunk at a Komsomal dance and struck a young Russian commissar in the jaw. To make matters worse, when the local militia tried to remove him from the dance floor, he kept yelling that all Russian Communists didn't know their asses from holes in the ground. Fred was charged the next day with hooliganism and given a three-year sentence of hard labour on the Stalin canal.

For some reason the genuine criminals—the thieves and murderers—had it easier than the political prisoners, and they usually sat around smoking, and stealing whatever they could get their hands on. Nearly everyone else was half-starved, and many died on their feet, the frozen corpses removed from the work site at the end of the day.

The Party said that petty crime was a product of capitalist society, and therefore common criminals could not be blamed for their condition. Fred thought the Party was crazy. He noticed that these thieves did whatever they wanted, and that they always had plenty of sausage, tobacco, and vodka. He watched them for days, and finally discovered one of their caches. One night he stole a gallon of their vodka and headed west into the marshes.

After several hours of trudging through frozen swamp and forest, he came upon a small hut, one of the shelters for travellers that are common in the Karelian woodlands. Soon Fred had a fire going in the stove, and with his jug in front of him was as comfortable as any king in any palace.

He liked nothing better than a conversation with himself. He could win any argument, point out emphatically the errors and stupidity of the people he knew, ridicule the crazy ideas of churches and politicians and make a few things straight with Sirkku. Tell her what he'd like to do with her.

"Ya, it's all bullshit," he muttered to his jug on the slab table. "Bullshit! Sirkku can go to hell! Five-Year Plan! Shock workers! It is all bullshit! My old man is bullshit!"

It was warm and dark in the little cabin. Fred felt at peace. He felt the alcohol seep through its thousand paths in his brain, and the fire excited and calmed him all at once. He was safe, confined by thick log walls and darkness, sheltered from the outside world. Each sip from his private chalice excited him more until he fell asleep from its ethers.

He woke after a long sleep and opened the door to the mid-day arctic light. His throat was dry and he could feel a cold sweat on the back of his neck. His hands shook, and where his clothing touched his body the skin hurt. The walls of the cabin, instead of comforting him, now closed in, choking him. Quickly he drank from the jug and left the hut.

He walked with his jug as the snow fell. His only fear was that he might finish the vodka before sleep came. On he went, sinking to his knees, and then he fell in the soft snow. He lay there like a broken scarecrow, and he drank from his precious jug. The warmth of his one and only trusted friend soon enveloped him, and the vodka put him to sleep in his shroud of falling snow.

The winter ended.

On a warm Sunday morning in June, Urho, little Pauli, and Sirkku's friend, Dr. Volkonsky, hiked to a stream a short distance from the farm, the place where the water flowed into Lake Onega. Pauli was chasing crayfish in a shallow pool, and the two men were standing on a bank above him, engaged in serious conversation.

"I don't know how you Russians keep track of things," Urho said.

The doctor moved his sailor's cap around on his head. He smiled, his black eyes creasing to mischievous slits.

"We don't," he said, "never have. Why bother the mind with organization when we can be fishing, and now in June there are no mosquitoes."

"The farm is a mess," Urho said. "I have been here three years, and every year things get worse. The loggers can't get an axe or a saw. I've been waiting seven months for a magneto to come from the Ford plant in Leningrad. And do they make such a thing as a spark-plug in this country?"

The doctor reached into his pocket and pulled out a jack-knife. "Pauli, climb up here. You won't catch many crayfish with your hands. I show you how to make a trap." He cut and trimmed a tree branch, slit the end, and blocked it open. "Follow me," he said to Paul. A crayfish, wider than the back of the doctor's hand, crawled in the shallows. The Russian stabbed his birch fork at the fish, releasing the block. "There, we have part of our supper," he said, holding the claw-snapping crayfish high in the air, caught in the green-wood pincers. He handed the stick to Paul who climbed carefully with it to show his father.

"Get some water in the pot," Urho said to the boy. "Put the fish in. We can prepare it later." He turned his attention back to Volkonsky. "I find it frustrating," Urho said. "We have no tools, and the cows have nothing to eat. Imagine, aspen leaves for silage."

"Better than pine needles," the doctor said. "A Russian is different from a Finn. You people come from America to do a job here, quickly, efficiently, and without tools you get things done, and don't even leave a mess when you finish. You seem to know what you want to do, and how to go about getting it done—practical is what I mean. A Russian gets bored with 'practical'. Last summer a Moscow scientist developed an impractical idea, a factory in Rostov—to make axle grease from grasshoppers. On the steppes are many grasshoppers, and the farmers need the axle grease. Great idea! So it didn't work? So what! Do you think it is practical to farm on a Karelian swamp? We Russians are content to watch you try, and we admire how much better you are at doing things."

Volkonsky sat down on the bank and looked at his cracked leather boots. At least they were leather. When they are gone who knows what he will get on his feet. He bobbed the fishing line in the deep water, looked at Urho, then at the boy poking his stick into the pot. "You know, Urho, you Finns are trying to do what the Mennonite Germans tried to do on the steppes during Catherine's time—show us how to farm. These German farmers did well for themselves, and the Russian peasant, sometimes scratching his small field with a stick, sometimes letting his wife do the scratching so he could get drunk, watched the Mennonites, admired their production, and maybe he was jealous. Where are the Mennonites now?"

"Hey! Wait! Wait! I have a fish!" He scrambled to his feet, and keeping the line tight, but not too tight, lifted the fish from the water, pulling it flapping up the bank to the top. "With Pauli's crayfish we now have enough for a feast," he said.

The doctor cleaned the fish. Urho made a cooking fire, then washed the handful of marble-sized potatoes he had brought with him. He placed them in the pot with fresh water and added an onion. Eva complained about potatoes—how the store could never get them, how they went soft because there was no place to store them, how much bigger they were at home. Yesterday Urho wanted to show her that it was possible to get potatoes. He walked three miles to a Karelian farm and talked the owner into selling him two kilos of his leftover seed potatoes.

The doctor put the pieces of fish into the pot. "So, you can't locate your brother-in-law—this Fred?" He watched Urho open a tightly twisted packet of brown paper, dump salt into the water, then carefully fold the paper and place it in his shirt pocket. "It's too bad if this Fred has been swallowed up. Russia has a big appetite, but you know, Urho, no matter where we are, in every case the earth swallows us all sooner or later."

Paul watched the chowder boil in the iron pot that was hanging from a tripod his father had fashioned from the green branches.

"You can stir the soup," Urho said to him. Paul wished his mother could be with them. Maybe there would be some chowder left to take home, and it might make her feel better. He didn't know last night when he put his mother's Pyrex saucepan into the cold water that it would break—he had only been trying to help. He didn't know it was a gift from Grandma Lempi. His mother cried and cried, and he didn't like that.

"Pauli, Pauli, Pauli," she had grieved, "we have so little, and now we have no saucepan. What good are your father's potatoes when there is nothing to fry them in? What would Lempi think?"

Because she worked in the Finnish store, Eva knew that only black bread and salt were in regular supply. She could sometimes count on rye flour, but wheat was a luxury. Rarely was there butter, or even margarine, and cooking oil was not always on hand. Dr. Volkonsky said that at least things weren't as bad as during the Revolution, when fats were so scarce that people cooked pancakes in glycerine.

Milk and eggs were sometimes delivered to the door by the Karelian farmer's wife, but Eva was never sure when. She could never figure out why they couldn't always get milk from their own dairy. Once or twice a year someone came to the farm selling apples and there were long line-ups. She never saw an orange or a banana, but one time the store did have a shipment of apple jelly powder. In the fall the Karelian farmer sold potatoes and cabbage—again the long line-ups.

On May Day, 1935, Eva worked outside the store in a kiosk from morning to night selling yard-goods. Always on May Day there was something special, and this year it was cotton prints, dozens and dozens of bolts. All day she cut and measured material. The line-up never ended. Eva was so busy she didn't see any of the parade or hear any speeches, just the band music. She didn't even see Paul marching with the young pioneers.

With all the perils of living in Karelia, it didn't seem possible that Eva would die from wearing an ill-fitting pair of felt boots.

Urho left the hospital in Kontupohja and tore off blindly into the forest. He leaned forward through the deep snow and snapping spruce boughs cut him. Blood and tears washed down his face. He didn't care if the branches poked his eyes out, and the more it hurt, the harder he tramped.

He didn't know or care where he was going, only the darker and farther away the better, deeper into the forest. What happened was so terribly stupid, and this made his loss hurt even more. No goddess could mean as much to him as Eva, his quiet Eva. Those fools! Stupid doctors! And all Urho could do was watch life drain from Eva in these few months.

Dr. Volkonsky had examined Eva's foot, Urho remembered: "How long has this been bothering you?" the doctor asked.

"About a month," Eva said, wincing at his touch. She bent forward and looked at her swollen heel. "I needed boots, and I got them—a pair big enough to fit Urho. There were none my size."

"The heel is infected, Eva, and I am afraid of blood poisoning. I will send you to the clinic in Kontupohja. At least that will get you out of these boots for awhile."

Urho remembered the hospital in Kontupohja. No

Urho remembered the hospital in Kontupohja. No matter what he had willed, he could change nothing, and there was no Lempi to go to.

"The pain shoots," Eva had said, "up my leg, like a toothache. Stay with me Urho. The nurses try to help, but they speak Russian. Stay, Urho."

"I will stay always," Urho had said.

"Don't let Pauli eat too much black bread—it gives him the runs. And, Urho—let my parents know." She had held out her hand, "Urho?" and he touched her fingers with both his hands and held them to his face. He stayed with her two more hours until she died.

Urho didn't know how long he raged through the bush, or how he got back to the farm. He found himself leaning on the red star gate, leaning against the bark-covered post, drained of his strength and his emotion.

The next few months Urho brooded in the dark gloom of the Karelian winter. If it had not been that Paul was with him at Sunu—that Paul needed him—Urho wasn't sure what he might have done. Those black days were a hole in his memory, a gap. Without this oblivion, he wondered if he could have survived.

Urho sat on the bank over the frozen stream. He held a pencil stub in his right hand, and wrote on a scrap of paper supported by a board on his knee.

To my Eva's parents, Dear Tenho,
I am sorry to hear that both of you are
not well. I haven't written for a long time
to anyone. Lempi sent me a letter with
Eva's obituary, to show me it was
published over there in Canada. I am
pleased that she sent it to the
paper. I also sent it to our own Karelian
newspaper, but for some reason it did
not appear. It may have been lost, or
somehow forgotten, I don't know. I've

had a carpenter make a marker for Eva's
grave. It is four feet high, and sixteen
inches thick, made out of one solid
piece of birch. It will be painted gray.
I haven't exactly thought of the wording
for it yet. After the land thaws, I will
take it there and also build a fence
around the grave and plant flowers....

He carefully folded the letter and put it in his vest pocket. It would soon be dark; he had better get back to the farm and see to Paul. Urho felt a strange peace as he walked the trail through the forest. Maybe it was the quiet of the night falling, or maybe because he had written the letter. Anyway, it was as if he had somehow been with Eva, and completed something, resolved something.

Urho walked on. There was only the scrunch of his boots on the crusted snow.

The little fence had stood two winters. Urho, with his son Paul, and Sirkku and the doctor, spent the May Day afternoon tending Eva's grave.

He never showed self-pity, but losing Eva scared him. It left some kind of hole in him, took part of who he was. Did he really want to visit the grave, or was it just that he thought he should? Eva was gone more than two years.... Could he be forgetting her?

Paul left the adults. He sat at the edge of the clearing on a log shaded by ferns and nettles. He had captured three fat slugs and now he watched them wiggle and curl in one of Urho's old tobacco tins. A slug slithered on clear sticky stuff, like spit, stuck to a mat of rotting leaves. The plump body pulsed in and out. Paul thought he could see short little teeth along the body, scraping in and out with the pulses, drawing little bits from the wet leaves. He could hear the adults talking.

"Kirov's assassination has changed everything," the doctor said. "Stalin thinks it was meant for him. It's not every day that a *Kirov* gets a bullet in the head. A Leningrad Party Chief is no small matter." The doctor rubbed his fingers on the peak of his sailor's cap, lifting it a moment off his head. His forehead creased. "Stalin thinks Hitler is everywhere—a conspiracy, spies in the Red Army, the Czarist officers. He thinks the Ukrainian Nationalists are in league with Hitler—all the cultures, anarchy of cultures, languages, so many factions. Stalin fears they will join the Hitler wolf pack already panting at his door."

"Urho, look." Sirkku raked the leaves from the enclosed grave. "Green shoots are coming through—the irises we planted."

"So they will survive," Urho said. He turned to Volkonsky. "Many are being arrested—heads of provincial committees, district committees, local committees—anyone who wants to reassert the Finnish language, even work brigade leaders at the farm."

"It's the damn Finns," Sirkku said, "They're always shooting their mouths off. They think they are the only ones who know anything."

"Scapegoats," the doctor said, looking a long moment at Sirkku, and then at Urho. "If the experiment fails, it cannot be the Party that is wrong. The Bolsheviks think the Party is the Holy of Holies. These party zealots are one thing, but they are not the ones who cause the failures, I think. The Party people work hard for their dreams." He stepped back from the little fence, and put his hands on his hips.

"The problem is the peasant." He paused. "The Russian *muzhik* is a special breed. Nothing is holy to this peasant, except land, and all the things are holy that help him grab and hold his land. He prays to God making deals for rain. For a farm the *muzhik* will marry any bitch. If he won't, he's not a *muzhik*. You don't mind my talk, eh Sirkku?"

"Go on, keep talking," she said.

"Before the Revolution I knew a *muzhik* from Smolensk who married a woman because she owned a cow. He drowned the woman in the well when he discovered that she could not bear him any sons. He wanted a son to carry on the farm. A *muzhik* will kill his own brother for land, and this love for land is why Stalin's collectivization is impossible. They who have lost their holdings, have sniffed their way into the government bureaus to grab what they can. Give a stupid one a whip and he will kill his horse. If he thinks he can get something from you, he will smile up at you, call you master, nod his head and agree with everything you say. And if you don't watch out, he will rob you, and report you to the Bolsheviks for wasting state property. Then he will meekly offer his services to the NKVD and the Secret Police will beat you as if you were a horse."

"Ya, the *muzhik*." Urho stirred whitewash with a stick, and then he brushed the thin paste on the little fence. "The *muzhik*. And not just the Russian—in every place there is that breed. They pick like magpies at a dead rabbit on the road." He dabbed more whitewash on the fence, watched it soak into the wood, then brushed the little bubbles of air smooth. "Like magpies they pick, and if a vehicle comes, the bird is gone. But it always comes back."

Urho even could see their faces, their noses crinkled, and the top lips sharply curled, showing the gums. Such people guarded their thoughts. They watched every moment, ever ready to pounce and pick. Nothing delighted them more, titillated them more, than to find disgrace in someone else. They hungered for the peep-show, revelled in sharing their disgust through gossip, and sated their lust stoning the victim. Urho detested such people—those who reported on others. Those anonymous snivellers who report to the police in secret. They had that breed in Canada.

Some whitewash slopped like a splat of bird droppings from the brush onto the ground, onto dead leaves at the base of the fence.

"Vigilance is needed," Sirkku said, leaning on her rake. "The Revolution is only twenty years old—it has many enemies. You know that, Urho. You know what it was like at home—I mean, back there in Canada. As you say, there were always those to pick holes—the class struggle is no Mid-summer picnic."

"But they are taking some of the best communists," Urho said. "Something is wrong."

A month later they took Urho.

Chapter Nineteen

They infected Vainola
And the Kalevalanders sickened
Of mysterious diseases,
Diseases never named before
Till the floors beneath them rotted,
Quilts above them soaked with sweating.

Kalevala, Runo 45

"You are Urho Maki?" The militia man was the dairy worker with the purple birthmark on his chin. Urho turned from his workbench, frowned, slowly nodded his head, and peered into the man's eyes.

I have a warrant for your arrest. Article 58 of the Criminal Code. Come with me."

"Arrest?" Urho felt a weakness in his knees, and he was dizzy, as if about to faint. "Article 58? What is this about?"

"Never mind!"

"Can I at least get my things? See my boy?"

"No," he said, "come with me now. The truck is waiting."

Lubyanka. A white cell. A light bulb. "Confess, you bastard, confess! Sign!" the fat man said. Sweat beaded the rolls of flesh on the back of the fat man's neck and on his jowls. Urho tried to read the piece of paper on the desk.

"What does it say? I don't read Russian."

"Sign it, you bastard!"

Article 58—counter-revolutionary activity. Everyone is Article 58, a train load of Article 58's. Ten years of hard labour. Lucky not to be shot.

At night the men are marshalled in the rail yards, ordered to squat like toads. Why don't they flee? Searchlights tie them down? Guard dogs? There are so many men and so few guards. But the toads are obedient. In lots of five the prisoners crowd into the first class car, a relic from czarist days, modified for prisoners.

Urho sits on the bottom bunk with five other Article 58's. Three more are stretched out flat on the platform midway up the wall. Two more men are pushed to the roof, crammed into the baggage shelf. Nine others on the floor at Urho's knees. Nine other cells in the car.

They're heading south and east, all night. At least it's cool at night. By noon next day the train begins to cross the steppes. The prison car is hot and Urho's cell is next to the latrine. The floor is wet, and the air is full of the stink of piss.

Urho remembers crossing the river in Matt Inhonen's wagon, climbing to the Coteau, the sweet air—he is four years old, riding on the river hills. The house with the diamond window on the porch door—homestead, sky, and hills—at night a speck of lantern light. His mother Senja dancing in the hall.

Prairie fire. Wet sacks swatting flames that jump the fire-guard. The fire makes its own wind—the wind controls. Sudden sweeping roars and snaps, the heat and smoke—so large against little people spanking the grass with wet sacks.

Lempi in the sauna. Cow horns—and blood.

The car is unbearably hot and Urho is thirsty. At three o'clock the guard comes with a pail and dumps salted herring on the floor, but no water. He says it is too much trouble to give them water. There are only two drinking cups—it would take too long—and if the prisoners drank water they would have to piss, and that would stink up the latrine in this heat.

The next morning the train arrived at Uralsk. For two hours Urho stood in line with the newcomers, while a half-literate trusty chewed on his pencil and put their names on the roll. A few feet away, an emaciated relic of a human being sat by a slop hole. A dirty brown wool cap covered his head down to his rheumy eyes. From what Urho could see of his face, it was blackish-brown, the skin peeling and ulcerated. He was covered in rags of all sorts and colours, all dulled with dirt, layer on padded layer of tears and patches.

This man protected his treasures on the ground: two fish heads, a few wet crusts of black bread, lumps of gruel, potato peels—all of this strained from the slop hole. Over a small fire he boiled water in a tin can and added pieces of his hoard. He stretched a withered hand from out of the folds of his sleeve and tugged at Urho's pantleg. His voice was a hoarse whisper: "The blood of all the prophets which was shed from the foundation of the world may be required of this generation."

In the middle of the night Urho woke and could not get back to sleep. When he tried to lift his head the room spun around him and he was short of breath, as if the platform above was pressed to his chest. He had been preoccupied with his arrest, with Lubyanka, with the train's heat and the piss stink, and his mind was full of the minute-by-minute calculations on how best to handle each new situation. All these things he could deal with. He had even visualized himself as that old madman by the little fire, and Urho had thought that even if it came to that, he could cope. He could cope with the strange snores on the platforms, and the stink of bodies in the crowded dorm.

But now, in the middle of the night, alone for the first time, he thought about Paul, and his body chilled. For the first time, he felt absolutely caged—the platform two feet above him, the prison camp , and the hundreds of miles that separated him from his son. He didn't know if he could cope with being unable to protect his son. His fear was even worse than when he had lost Eva. Then, he had known that no one could help Eva anymore. Then, at least, he had been driven by the power of his grief. Now he had no power—he was on his back, flat on a board, caged. His son was alive, and needed someone. Sirkku was with him. But what if something happened to Sirkku?

Chapter Twenty

And old Väinämöinen wondered:
"Has my final ruin fallen,
Has my day of doom come on me
In the haunts of Tuonela,
In the caverns of the dead?"

Kalevala, Runo 16

Pikku butchered a yearling at Lempi's place. She collected the blood pumping from the steer's gashed throat. She brought the pan into the house and at the kitchen table she stirred the blood, adding snow to cool it. She would make bloodbread, big round loaves like giant doughnuts, and string them on a broomstick hung on the rafters in the attic. She'd make some loaves for Pikku to take home with him. He liked to break up lumps of bloodbread and put them in his soup.

Ya, and maybe a cake. Why not, she thought. I am seventy-five tomorrow. Why not make a cake with the blood, like Father used to with the rye flour and suet from the kidney.

As she stirred she read a letter that Sirkku had sent her. It was Urho's letter, crowded words carefully written in pencil on a scrap of coarse paper. She bent, squinting in the faint light.

> *Certainly, Paul, you may go to Grandma Lempi's if it can be arranged.*
>
> *I don't think I will be freed for some time. I am innocent, but it looks as if that makes no difference. It might be better for you to go to Canada. If you do go, send your letters to Sirkku. The mail from abroad might not get to this camp. I haven't been well lately. I've often*

had a fever, and feel very weak. It is hoped this
weakness will pass. Be a good boy, Paul.
Possibly we will see each other again
someday. Remember that I am innocent. I have
always fought for the Soviet Union, and eve-
rybody knows that—you can walk with your
head held high. This camp has over nine hun-
dred prisoners—Ukrainians, Jews, Germans,
Poles, a few Chinese, Tartars, Russians, and us
Finns. I received the envelopes. Send some
more, and writing paper.

bye bye, Pauli,
your father,
Urho

The door opened. Pikku stomped snow off his boots
and hung up his coat. "Have you got something for sharpening
the knife, Lempi?" She got the stone from the cupboard drawer.
He wiped blood from his knife and sat at the table, sharpening,
watching Lempi stir the blood.

"So," he said, "you read the letter again?"

Lempi nodded. She had asked Pikku to write to the
government or whoever could do something to get Paul out
from that prison land. But Pikku is stubborn. He knows what
she wants but he won't admit that Russia is the work of the
Devil.

She kept stirring even though the blood had cooled,
waiting for Pikku to give in. It is not hard for an old woman to
wait.

He put the stone away and walked to the door. He put
on his coat, opened the door and then turned to Lempi—"I
suppose something could be done. Ya, but with the war it won't
be easy getting him out, and it will be harder than ever if Hitler
invades the Soviet Union. Maybe I could write to the Red
Cross." Lempi stopped stirring, then folded the letter, and put
it away in the cupboard drawer.

Sirkku heard the announcement blaring over the street micro-phones as she was eating her lunch at the communal kitchen: *"The Fascists have invaded the Motherland. Everyone report to the Assembly Hall immediately! Repeat—everyone to the Assembly Hall —immediately!"*

Sirkku ran to the school where she saw the children assembling outside the building.

"Pauli, did you hear?"

"Yes," he said. "The teacher said we will drown Hitler in the Atlantic Ocean."

In the railcoach no seat was empty. Some people stood. Sirkku hugged her bundle close to her lap. The train must hurry, she thought. What did the commissar say? Is it possible that Leningrad could fall? Funnel all evacuees to Leningrad, he said, then move the people east to safety. She would stay with Volkonsky to defend the city, but Paul would have to leave.

The doctor talked to the boy. "This retreat is a page from *War and Peace*. Mother Russia swallowed Napoleon, then spit him out like so much vomit." Ya, Sirkku thought. Maybe. The commissar said burn everything. Leave nothing of value behind. Nothing for Hitler. Nothing for Mannerheim.

Leningrad was covered in a gray haze verging on rain. Sirkku, Volkonsky, and Paul hurried from the train at Finland station to catch a trolley crossing the bridge over the Neva. Paul was to be on the other side of the city at Moscow station by five o'clock. They still had time to see the sights.

"I want to see the *Bronze Horseman,* Peter the Great on his rearing horse," Paul said. They stepped off the trolley at the Admiralty building and walked to Decembrist Square. A crowd of men and women shovelled earth ten feet high around the granite base of the statue. Paul could not see Peter the Great. The statue was padded with rock-wool and crated over like a building under construction.

"They cover all the statues," Volkonsky said. "Protect them from the bombs." A column of Red Army soldiers marched past on the street. The workers raised their shovels and the soldiers responded by holding their bayonets high.

Tanks rumbled over the cobblestones in the big square in front of the Winter Palace. Volkonsky pointed to the marble column in the centre of the square. "Alexander's Column," he said. "See at the top? The statue, St. Michael the Archangel." It held a cross, and its marble head bent forward appearing to look down on them and on the tanks parading out the gates.

It was time for Paul to leave. A trolley took them the length of Nevsky Prospekt all the way to Moscow station. A trainload of children—orphans and the offspring of state criminals, departed for Moscow, and then to a corrective labour brick-works camp, seventy kilometres east of the Capital.

A tall boy with a broken nose was the leader in Paul's dormitory. His name was Slingshot. The second morning Paul was in camp this group was loitering by the mess hall when an old man came out of the building, walking cautiously. He had his ten-ounce ration of black bread tucked inside his grayish shirt. Slingshot confronted him, his index and middle fingers poised at the man's eyes.

"I'll gouge your eyes out, you shit!" he said.

A small boy crawled in behind the man. Slingshot pushed him and he fell backwards over the boy. Slingshot sat on him, tore his shirt, and grabbed the bread. He tore up the loaf and tossed the bits around him in the yellow dirt. They left the man crawling on his hands and knees to retrieve his bread. Everyone laughed except Paul. Slingshot noticed that.

That evening a nurse came into the dormitory. She wore the red scarf of the young pioneers, and as soon as she gathered the boys together, began talking to them about new soviet morality. Slingshot smiled at her, and then waved his arm. From the top bunk two boys piled down on the woman, tumbling her to the floor. Boys were all over her, pinning her arms, spreading her legs, tearing her blouse off, reaching under her dress. Slingshot yelled "Lift her upside-down." Paul could watch no more.

"You are chicken," Slingshot said to him.

When they let go of her, Paul thought she would run to the commissar and they would be punished. But she didn't do that. She stood at the door, straightened herself as best she could, and spoke. Paul could not believe his ears. "I will ignore this," she said. "You are not responsible for the remnants of capitalist morality that create such behaviour." She asked them if they needed anything? Was anyone sick? She was there to help them, and surely they could behave better. Everyone must sacrifice because of the war, but the young must come first, she said, because the young were the future.

The next Monday the boys were assigned to cart away sludge from the latrines. On a wagon they hauled a large overflowing barrel to a deep pit on the outskirts of the camp. Paul was helping tilt the barrel when Slingshot pushed him towards the hole. Paul's foot slipped on the wet clay and he reached out and grabbed Slingshot's arm. The bully's feet slid from under him and he fell into the pit. Paul was at the edge, hanging on to the wagon wheel. He saw Slingshot disappear in the bubbling muck ten feet below.

After this, the other boys wanted Paul to be their leader, but he made no move to lead. He preferred to watch the men work at the brick ovens. The boys left him alone.

Paul helped stack the bricks in the great piles being readied to transport to Moscow. When the trucks came he helped with the loading. One day a driver wearing a peaked cap called to him: "How would you like to drive the truck to the next pile?"

"Me? Would you really let me drive?" Paul asked.

"Sure, why not? How old are you?"

"Fifteen."

He jumped into the cab and drove to the pile of bricks. When he got there, a slender woman in a uniform walked towards him. He thought he was in trouble.

"Are you Paul Maki?" she asked.

"Yes."

"Come with me," she said.

Paul was given a bundle of new clothes and sent to the

bathhouse. He was told nothing until he was on the train heading across Russia to Vladivostock. He was on his way to Canada.

Paul did not know that his father had crossed Russia on the same railroad just days before. A large contingent of prisoners from Uralsk was transferred to open a camp in the gold fields of the Kolyma in northeast Siberia.

Chapter Twenty-one

"I was small, and lost my father,
Very small, and lost my mother,
Father died and mother died,
And my whole clan perished with them."

Kalevala, Runo 34

Paul arrived at the Dunblane station late in the evening during a snowstorm. Old Pikku stood on the platform, his shoulders hunched, the snow swirling about him. The boy stepped from the train. He clutched with both hands the handle of his small black suitcase. Pikku reached for it. "Do you remember me?" he said. The boy quickly jerked the case closer to his body. "Maybe we go into the station," Pikku said. "Warm up before we set out for the farm, okay?"

The conductor was at the wicket with the station agent, examining a way bill. The clock on the wall chimed ten times. Pikku warmed his hands at the pot-bellied stove.

Paul stepped towards him and addressed Pikku quietly in Finn: "You take me to Grandma Lempi? That is right?"

"Yes Pauli, we go now, okay. The storm may get worse."

It was very dark, and they had to cover their faces because of the driving snow. They'd gone what seemed a long way when the horses balked. Pikku had to get down off the sleigh which was in a high drift, and the horses floundered, up to their bellies in snow. Pikku tugged at their bridles, swore at the horses, their massive heads bobbing, and suddenly the wind increased. It whistled and howled.

"What's that screaming?" Paul shouted. He dreaded unknown sounds, hated not knowing where they came from.

"That whistling must come from the wind blowing through the broken windows. I think we are by the old hall. Last summer they broke the windows." Pikku yelled through the wind. "Some bad kids." He climbed back into the sleigh, held his mitt under his arm and wiped the wet snow from his eyes with his bare hand. The horses had calmed down and they pulled the sleigh through the drift.

Then the wind blew stronger. Behind the hall an outhouse door flapped open, strained on its rusty hinges, and flapped shut once more. The horses reared, then tore off at a gallop. Pikku gave them their heads. They ran more than a mile before they slowed.

The horses pulled into a yard. Pikku got off the sleigh to unhitch the team. "Slide open the barn door, Pauli. Jerk it hard to break loose the ice." The horses, still in their harness, the lines dragging behind them, walked into the wide stall in the barn. Pikku lit a lantern that hung from a harness peg. Paul saw puffs of steam lifting off the bodies of the big horses. "Before I bed them down, I take you to the house," Pikku said.

What Paul remembered of the cold porch was the smell. It had a sharp smell, a mixture of sour milk and barn that was pleasant to him. A memory. They brushed snow from their pantlegs, shared a broom to sweep the bits of ice clinging to their felt boots, then swept snow from each other's back.

Pikku saw that Lempi had made ice cream—the bucket was on the floor in the corner. He wondered if the boy remembered the taste of ice cream. He opened the door to the kitchen. Lempi stood in the middle of the floor wringing a dish towel in her hands.

"Oh, *voi, voi!* Is this Paul? Come in, come in. Don't worry about a bit of snow." She saw the boy hesitate, draw back, his hands tightening on the handle of his suitcase. She stepped back, her thick felt socks padding softly on the floor. Lempi gestured a welcome with her arms, drew him into the room. She went to the cupboard, selected the biggest loaf of bread, and a knife from the drawer.

"Ya, that is quite a storm," Pikku said, flapping his

leather mitts on his legs. Sniffing deeply, he looked at the loaves on the counter, and then at Paul. "Ya, the fresh bread sure smells good."

Hanging on a hook from the ceiling, the gas lamp hissed and flared. Its white light added to the warmth coming from the kitchen stove. On the table Lempi set a plate stacked with slices of bread, a pot of strawberry jam and fresh butter. Paul buttered each slice, spread jam on every one, and drew the slices close to him. When he finished eating he spoke.

"The horses ran away on us."

"Ya," Pikku said. He hadn't moved from his place at the door. "The team spooked from the wind howling by the hall."

"Ah," Lempi said. "Ghosts—the devil is angry because the government closed his hall."

"Oh sure. Ghosts!" Pikku said. "Always ghosts!"

"No, this is true. I remember after the big rain in July. I picked saskatoons until dark in Mukari's coulee. Walking home past the hall I saw a light burning in the broken window, and I heard fiddle music, and laughing. Didn't I tell you, Pikku, the devil lives under that dance-floor."

"Ah, I go to the barn."

The storm had let up. He unharnessed the team, fed them, then skied the half mile to his shack. What next would happen? He remembered how it had been, before the people went to Karelia. So many had been confident of the coming Revolution, and then the Depression dragged on so long that doubts sprang up even in Pikku's mind. He remembered the hall packed with people in the good old days, then how the numbers began dwindling. Three years ago Finland and Russia went to war against each other—the Winter War. It broke his heart to see his countrymen desert the hall, and the Revolution. The Royal Canadian Mounted Police came to his shack, took him in the police car to the hall, and put a padlock on the door, "By order of the Government of Canada." He was powerless to do anything. All that was left of the Finnish Organization to voice a protest was Hilja Mukari and himself. A long time ago they were strong with men like Taisto Maki and Matt Inhonen. When they built the hall the people would have laughed Lempi's imaginings out of the hills. It was not like that now. Half the people believed there were ghosts under the floor, and the other half wanted to believe it.

One morning in April, Pikku and Hilja came to question Paul about the events in Karelia. Lempi served them coffee, then she went to feed the chickens. The meeting had started when she came back into the house, and after washing the eggs in the sink, she sat in her rocker and listened.

Paul sat at the table with this strange pair—Pikku with the cigarette pinched in his little mouth, and fat Hilja. Pikku struck a match, lit his cigarette, and puffed. " So many went to Karelia, Pauli. We knew this exodus of our best young people would weaken us here. You know, each time someone returns, the gossips celebrate at the barbershop. They sneered and laughed at us. Hilja and I are the only ones left in the hills who will admit to having been a red in the first place. What did happen in Karelia, Pauli?"

Hilja snapped at the boy. "You have disgraced the Movement," she said. "Why do you pamper him, Pikku? He has some explaining to do."

Pikku said nothing.

"What about the lies?" Hilja continued. "Otto Jukola spreads stories that in Russia you must sleep with your boots on if you still want them in the morning."

"Yes, in the corrective labour camps," Paul answered. "There are thieves. But not outside the prison camps. Not when we lived at Sunu." Lempi rose from her chair and filled their cups.

"Was there coffee in Karelia?" Pikku asked.

"No, never coffee unless a parcel came from here. But what I really liked in Russia was the tea. We drank it in glasses. The tea here is not as good."

Pikku put a lump of sugar in his mouth. He tilted his

cup, carefully spilling hot coffee into his saucer. He brought it to his lips, and slurped. "In Karelia, did they speak the Finn?" he asked, the words static, each one stressed.

"Yes," Paul said, "Especially at the beginning. When we went to Karelia, everything was Finn for us. We had our own Finnish store with luxury items—apples, and even chocolate sometimes. Around the time Mother died, things began changing. The store was closed, and the Finnish newspaper, the school. I was the only Finn in my grade who passed the first year at the Russian school."

Pikku settled back. He had heard enough. The horrors were true.

"These arrests," Pikku asked, "Your father—Urho. What is Comrade Stalin up to?"

Hilja started in her chair. She glared at Pikku, and her broad hands gripped the edge of the table.

"I don't know," Paul said. "Aunt Sirkku has a friend, a doctor. He and father held many discussions about Stalin. At school we had long lectures on Kirov's assassination—how it grieved Comrade Stalin. Dr. Volkonsky in his discussions with father hinted that maybe Stalin had something to do with Kirov's shooting."

Hilja Mukari pushed away from the table. "How dare you mention such counter-revolutionary garbage!" she said, hitting the table with her fist.

"Easy Hilja," Pikku said, "Let the boy talk."

"I did not understand much of their conversations," Paul said. "Something about ancient life force, and Asiatic darkness—something cruel and basic deep in Russia's history. The doctor said the same thing would happen to Hitler as happened to Napoleon."

"One last question," Pikku said. "What did you like the best during your time in Karelia?"

"School," Paul said. "Everyone took school seriously, not like here. We studied about all countries, even studied myths such as the Karelian *Kalevala,* and mathematics. I think now, I would like to go to a big school somewhere."

The next Saturday morning Paul went with Pikku and Lempi for an outing. The Municipal Council had asked Pikku to investigate Matt Inhonen. "People are saying he is half-dead," Pikku said. "He tries to move that ship to the river." The morning was more like November than the middle of April. The clouds were solid and lumpy, a cold blue-gray, like before a snowstorm. The dead grass smelled of winter moulds. A hard wind blew dust in Paul's eyes, and into his nose, making him sneeze.

On the flat they saw a winch rigged to the big boat. They walked to it. A horse lay dead, still harnessed to the winch cable, and Matt Inhonen was on his knees fumbling with the bridle. He pulled at the horse's head, as if trying to wake it. The shipbuilder reminded Paul of the clay pits—the man Slingshot's gang had robbed of bread, the same vacant look. Matt Inhonen pulled at the bridle, repeatedly, as if in a ritual.

Lempi knelt at the horse's head, put her hands on Matt's, drawing them from the bridle, and held Matt Inhonen in her arms, rocking slowly back and forth. She glanced up at the name painted on the ship. *Sontianen.* It did not surprise Lempi that a Finn would spend his life building, and then trying to drag this huge ship to the river with his bare hands. It did not surprise her that he called the ship *Sontianen*—a 'dung beetle'. Wasn't that just like a Finn—a great ship he builds, and calls it 'Dung Beetle.'

Yes, Lempi thought, not the smallest, not the greatest—it's for Swedes to brag.

Chapter Twenty-two

"Grant us this at least, O Lord,
In the future, true creator,
That the way be clear with markers,
Blazes cut along the pathway
Pointing in the right direction
For this staunch and manly nation."

Kalevala, Runo 46

That August Paul decided he should move far away.

"I have cousins there," he told Lempi. He sat on a stool, watching her weave. "I can go to High School in Vancouver."

Lempi squinted from the sun shining through the east window onto her loom. She rubbed her fingers gently on the warm rug—blue, green, yellow, red, black. How much more of this world does he want to see, she wondered. She sighed, brushed lint from her sweater, and walked into the kitchen. She cut two slices of *pulla* and placed them on the table along with some butter. "Come Pauli," she said, and then sat in her rocker.

She wondered what was so special about the *pulla?* Always she served a little at a time. In Finland wheat flour was precious. Imagine, this *pulla* is always like something precious.

Before breakfast she had walked out to the slough in the pasture. She did something she hadn't done since she was a girl in Finland. She walked bare-footed, making prints with her toes in the black mud along the shore. During the thirties there had been water in that slough only a few weeks after spring run-off. Now the pasture was green. She saw plants she had not seen before, or had forgotten. She saw carpets of fern-like plants with rows of paired serrated leaves. She saw thousands of little white flowers, like tiny daisies. Paul had shown her these flowers in a schoolbook. He called them many-flowered asters. By the slough there was a sister flower, not as many, but the same size and shape as the white aster. These flowers had violet-blue petals that radiated from yellow centres. She had seen golden tansy and misty patches of baby's breath. She saw willow shoots by the slough, as thin as a pencil, reaching ten feet. And mushrooms. She hadn't seen mushrooms since she left Finland. Could she remember which ones were safe to eat? Through the long Depression years the Coteau earth held this life, patiently, waiting for the rain.

The wild flowers were special to her, just like the *pulla*. Make the *pulla* just so, serve it quietly, sparingly, always the same. Then she thought of Paul—that he was somehow like the *pulla*. She saw in the boy her wish to keep tradition alive.

Paul spread the soft butter on the bread, and he ate. "Something in the taste," he said. "Something secret in the taste."

"Ya," Lempi said, "Maybe that is only cardamom seed." She ran her fingers along the armrest of her chair and slowly rocked back and forth. Paul played with the table knife, reflecting sunlight off the blade, splashing it on the walls, on the chrome trimmings of the new McClary stove. Lempi saw how his hand shook. A boy of sixteen shouldn't shake like that, she thought. What sorrows he must know. He knows already what it takes a lifetime for others to learn. He knows he cannot have the *Sampo*. Maybe that is good he knows. This century no one values what he cannot see. No one values what he cannot control—the things where we have no more say than do the purple aster flowers.

"What do you think, Lempi, should I go to Vancouver?"

"Oh, my boy, how should I know? Only you can know." She gripped her puffy hands together, rolled her apron into a ball and then unrolled it, smoothed it. "What do I know about the world here, or in this Vancouver?"

"I guess I will go," he said.

"Whatever you think, Pauli. But that's enough of this for now. Maybe we get Pikku to take us to the river tomorrow and we can have a picnic. Maybe you catch a fish."

"Father took me fishing many times."

"Ya, Pauli—you miss your parents. The life has been hard for you. Maybe for all of us. You know, it is not easy to be a Finn. Luxury—that is for Swedes. Maybe that's why your father was a communist. Finland had no king. The Finn likes to be the underdog, even old *Väinämöinen*, ya, and always stubborn, we Finns are stubborn. Seven hundred years ago, when the Swedes conquered Finland, the army brought a bishop with them, set out baptizing the people, village by village. The men, women, and children were gathered on the river bank, and any Finn who refused to be dunked had his head chopped off. Some refused—it is not uncommon for a Finn to lose his head rather than have to give an inch."

"Ya," Paul said, "maybe that is what bothers me."

"But you know, Pauli, on that river bank one Finn suddenly charged at the bishop, and before they could do anything, he swung his sabre, and cut off the bishop's head. That is a Finn," Lempi said.